'Are you by any cha...

The deep, slightly drawling tones were horribly familiar. Laura was well aware of the questioner's identity before she spun round and faced Martin Kent. 'Yes, I am. Why do you ask?'

'Because I'm going there too.' He grinned suddenly and his whole face changed. 'As you must know, Nurse—er—Marsden, I haven't been a consultant very long and the old habits die hard. I find I miss the convivial atmosphere of the Monk and occasionally indulge myself.' He paused and then added casually, 'Since it's your birthday, you might care to join me.'

For a moment Laura was too astonished to speak. He had, with what she considered his usual arrogance, taken her agreement for granted and, since the lights changed at that moment, had actually thrust his arm through hers and was steering her across the road. And as they walked along together her sense of humour began to assert itself as she pictured the faces of her two friends when she arrived with a man she was known to dislike so intensely.

She'd never live it down!

Clare Lavenham was born and brought up in London, but she has spent most of her life in Suffolk. She has a son and a daughter who was a nurse at the London Hospital. She has written articles, short stories and one-act plays, but it was because of her work as a hospital librarian that she turned to writing Medical Romances. She gets her backgrounds from her library work and consults various medical friends when necessary. Her favourite occupations, apart from writing, are walking in the country and gardening.

Previous Titles

WEB OF MEMORIES
YOUNG DOCTOR LATHAM
THE NEW SURGEON AT ST FELIX

LOVE YOUR NEIGHBOUR

BY

CLARE LAVENHAM

MILLS & BOON LIMITED
ETON HOUSE   18–24 PARADISE ROAD
RICHMOND   SURREY   TW9 1SR

First published in Great Britain 1991
by Mills & Boon Limited

© Clare Lavenham 1991

Australian copyright 1991
Philippine copyright 1991
This edition 1991

ISBN 0 263 77219 5

Set in 10½ on 12½ pt Linotron Palatino
03-9104-45087
Typeset in Great Britain by Centracet, Cambridge
Made and printed in Great Britain

CHAPTER ONE

THE restaurant was a popular one and very crowded, but Laura had booked a table and the three girls did not have to queue.

'I hope we shan't have to wait long to get served,' she said as they sat down. 'I'm on duty at two o'clock.'

Jenny and Anita exchanged smug glances. 'No need for us to worry about the time,' Jenny remarked. 'We're free all day.'

'Don't rub it in!' Laura picked up the menu. 'Anyway, I'm lucky to have a free morning on my birthday and it's an absolute miracle that you two are able to share my special lunch. What are you going to eat? Do choose something wildly extravagant because that legacy my aunt left me came through yesterday and I'm feeling rich.'

'I thought you said it was quite a small one——' Jenny began, but Anita interrupted.

'You shouldn't be spending it on us. It's we who should be treating you on your birthday.'

'Don't be daft! What does it matter who pays? I just happen to have the lolly at the moment, that's all.' Laura bent her sleek blonde head over the list of tempting dishes. 'I'm going to have smoked salmon for starters.'

The friendship was long-standing—going back to their days at the Nurse Education Centre—and its success was perhaps due to the fact that they were all so different. Laura was an only child whose parents—both teachers—worked in grammar schools, but Jenny's father kept a sub-post office and she had numerous brothers and sisters. Anita, the daughter of a college lecturer, was a complete contrast to both of them. Half African, she had the black hair and melting brown eyes of her mother's people, and her skin was the colour of milk chocolate. She was a staff nurse in a surgical ward, whereas Jenny and Laura were taking a midwifery course in the big new maternity block at Wickenfield Hospital.

'What about the other half of your aunt's legacy?' Jenny asked when they had given their order. 'When will you be able to take possession of her house?'

'Any time I like!' Laura was radiant, her blue eyes sparkling. 'It's legally mine now and as soon as I can find time to go round the second-hand shops and buy odds and ends of furniture I shall move into my very own home.'

'Didn't your aunt leave any furniture?'

'Oh, yes, but it was terribly old-fashioned without being in the least antique, if you know what I mean. I got a house clearance man to take it all away. I shall just furnish my bedroom and the sitting-room to begin with.'

'I suppose you know how lucky you are,' Anita

said wistfully. 'If Gavin and I managed to get a place like that we'd be over the moon.'

Laura gave her a sympathetic glance. 'Sometimes I feel a bit guilty because everything seems to be going my way just now,' she confessed.

'Guilty? You must be joking!'

Jenny was not listening. She had pushed back a handful of her brown curls and lodged them behind an ear, her eyes on a table by the window. 'Don't look now, but I think there's one of our ex-customers over there, Laura. Portway's the name and she had twins. Remember her?'

'Vaguely. What's so special about her? No doubt Wickenfield is full of our ex-patients.'

'But they don't all lunch at the Granville. I remember this one particularly because I was assisting at the birth, but I had hardly anything to do because Martin Kent delivered the twins himself and there was a bit of trouble with the smaller one. Mrs Portway was tremendously grateful and kind of hung on to his every word while she was in hospital.'

'That's not likely to make me want to remember her,' Laura said tartly.

Anita looked up from the avocado and Parma ham she was enjoying. 'I can't think why you don't like Martin Kent. Most people seem to.'

'Perhaps that's why.'

'What sort of a reason do you call that?'

'I don't know and I don't care.' Laura smiled to take the sting out of her words. 'And, what's more, I refuse to discuss Martin Kent at my birthday lunch.'

Jenny had been continuing to stare at the two young women at the window table. One was slim and smartly dressed and the other was wearing a shapeless maternity dress. She now drew attention to them again.

'I should think Mrs Portway's friend is one of our future customers—and pretty soon by the look of her. The poor girl's the size of a house.'

In spite of her declared lack of interest, Laura glanced across. 'She doesn't have to be coming to us. She might be having the baby at a private maternity home, or even in her own house. Whichever it is, I agree she won't have long to wait.'

For the rest of the meal they talked about other things, but regularly coming back to Laura's inheritance. Neither Anita nor Jenny was interested in the ten-year-old Rover car which also belonged to their friend now, since neither of them drove, and Laura did not mention it either. Secretly, she found it a little embarrassing. It had matched the personality of the sedate and spinsterish Miss Mary Marsden, but it would look ridiculous in the hospital car park among the battered sports cars of the housemen, and the Minis and Metros of those nurses who could afford to run a car.

Laura intended to sell it one day, when she had scraped up enough money for something more exciting, but in the meantime she would need it for driving to the hospital from her new home in a small village which was almost a suburb of Wickenfield.

'I hope they won't be long bringing our coffee,' she said, looking down at her watch. 'There's not much time left, and Sister is on duty this afternoon so it's more than my life is worth to be late.'

The coffee came at that moment, strong and black with a jug of cream, and she poured it out. As they sipped appreciatively, enjoying the last moments of luxury, Laura felt a tap on her shoulder.

'Excuse me——' It was the slim dark young woman whom Jenny had referred to as Mrs Portway. 'You're a nurse from the maternity unit at the hospital, aren't you? I remembered you at once because of your lovely hair. Please, please can you help?'

'There's another maternity nurse over there,' Laura said, indicating Jenny. 'What's the matter, then?'

'The most awful thing's happened—my friend has gone into labour, right here at the Granville!'

'Oh, dear—I'm afraid that must have spoilt lunch for both of you!' Laura tried to calm Mrs Portway's agitation by taking it lightly. 'I don't suppose she's likely to give birth right away, so the best thing you can do is to get her home as quickly as possible.'

'You don't understand—this is urgent. It's Lucy's third baby and she was terribly quick with the other two. It wasn't due until next week or we wouldn't have come here, but she's had a worrying time lately and I thought it might cheer her up. Do please come and see her.'

'Of course I will.' Laura gave her a reassuring smile and finished her coffee quickly. 'You take your friend to the ladies' room and I'll join you there. Then I'll do my best to assess the situation and tell you what I think you'd better do. OK?'

'Oh, thank you. I knew you'd help.'

'I'd begun to think I was invisible,' Jenny complained when Mrs Portway had hurried away. 'It's funny how people always remember blue-eyed blondes, but brown hair and hazel eyes make no impact at all. Shall I come with you or do you want to handle this on your own?'

'You have to be joking! *Of course* I want you to come.'

Jenny and Anita reached the cloakroom first, since Laura was delayed by paying the bill. She found them doing their best to reassure the mother-to-be, who was clutching her back and groaning, her lank mouse-coloured hair framing a face which glistened with sweat.

'Looks like you'd better phone for an ambulance, Laura,' Jenny said in an undertone. 'It's a lot more urgent than we thought.'

'Did you manage to time the contractions?'

'It's hardly necessary. You can see for yourself how frequent they are.'

'For goodness' sake, *do* something!' Mrs Portway was wringing her hands.

Laura abandoned her deliberately calm manner and acted decisively. 'I've got my car parked round the back. It'll be much quicker to use that than to call an ambulance, and I'm going straight to the hospital anyway. I'll go and get it while you bring Lucy downstairs and out by the back entrance.'

'See you at the pub tonight, then?' Jenny said in a hasty aside. 'You must come and have a birthday drink.'

Laura nodded and set off at speed, groping for her car keys as she went. Her ancient Rover was parked in a far corner, but she got it started quickly and moved it as close to the door as possible. By the time the patient and her escort had arrived she was ready for them.

'What's your other name?' she asked as Lucy squeezed her bulk into the passenger seat.

'Goring.' She paused to stifle a groan and then continued, 'What about my case? It's all packed ready but I haven't got it with me.'

'The hospital will provide what you need and perhaps your husband can bring it when he comes. Is your friend going to phone him?' There was a pause which Laura interpreted as being given up to the endurance of another pain, but, as they sped through back-streets on their way to the huge range of buildings which comprised Wickenfield hospital, Lucy Goring answered her question.

'My husband is away at the moment but my mother is staying with me. I expect she'll bring the case.'

You'd think the man would want to know about the imminent arrival of another baby, Laura reasoned, wherever he was, but she made no comment. Instead she asked, 'Do you want a boy or a girl?'

'I've got two boys so this one had better be a girl.' Another contraction tore at her body and she relapsed into silence except for the small uncontrollable sounds which she had been making intermittently all the time.

Laura left it at that. She had sensed discord from the moment that Mr Goring had been mentioned, but this was certainly not the time for prying into Lucy's private life. They had nearly reached the hospital now. It sprawled across a large area on the outskirts of the town, with the maternity block standing up straight and tall at one end.

It was nearly two o'clock and Laura was uncomfortably aware of her own need for haste. Unfortunately everything now seemed to move at a slow rate. She managed to get Lucy safely to a seat while she asked the porter to telephone up to Cecilia Ward to warn them that an urgent case was on the way. Then she had to find a wheelchair for her patient and wait while the lift became available, which again seemed to take valuable seconds.

Eventually it arrived with a soft whisper of sound and the wide doors slid smoothly back. First to emerge was an orderly pushing an empty wheelchair. He was followed by two hospital cleaners and a tall man in a charcoal-grey suit wearing the tie of a big London teaching hospital. He looked deep in thought, his dark head a little bowed. His grey eyes had an inward look and he was slightly frowning. Martin Kent, the junior gynaecological consultant, was considered by most of the nurses to be outrageously good-looking, but a few of them—including Laura—suspected that he was rather too well aware of the fact.

As Laura waited politely until he was clear of the lift, Lucy gave a little squeak of excitement.

'Martin! Oh, I'm so glad you're here—you promised you'd look after me.'

His dark brows rose fractionally. 'Surely you aren't due until next week?'

'I've started early. Oh, God——' A fierce contraction silenced her.

'This baby will born in the lift if we don't hurry.' Martin led the way back into the spacious interior. 'I can't imagine how *you* got involved with this, Nurse—er—Marsden, but explanations can wait. The important thing is to get Mrs Goring to the delivery-room as quickly as possible.'

Someone else would certainly require an explanation, Laura thought apprehensively as they were whisked up to the third floor. Sister Leggett would want to know all the details and it could almost be guaranteed that she wouldn't approve of any of them. Unfortunately there seemed to be very little she approved of these days.

But, if she was astonished to see a new patient

arriving in the care of a consultant and one of her nurses—who was wearing smart navy trousers and a scarlet jacket—she made no comment at the time. There were more important matters to be attended to. Gratefully Laura disappeared into the locker-room, from which she soon emerged correctly clad in a blue-and-white striped dress with her SRN belt round her slim waist and a neat pleated cap hiding most of her hair.

'I'm glad to see you suitably dressed, Nurse Marsden,' Sister said acidly.

She was a thin woman, very close to retirement age, who looked as though she had permanent indigestion. She was usually kind to the patients—provided that she didn't feel they were making an unnecessary fuss—and she loved small babies, but her nurses were generally glad when she was off duty and Diana Mildmay, the senior midwife, was in charge of them.

'I'm sorry I was a bit late, Sister,' Laura said glibly.

As she embarked on the whole story she was uneasily aware that it sounded weak. She had let herself be influenced a little by Mrs Portway's panic, she now realised. It would have been better to call an ambulance and then get off to the hospital herself as soon as possible. That way she wouldn't have been late.

'You certainly seem to have acted rather impulsively,' she was told when she had finished, 'and there was really no need for you to take so much on yourself. However, you're here now and we certainly need you this afternoon. Three of our mothers have come in early.'

The way she said it made it seem as though she believed the mothers had done it on purpose, yet Laura was aware that she hadn't intended that. It was probably because she was so old, she thought charitably, and the job was becoming too much for her.

'What would you like me to do, Sister?' she asked.

'You'd better get scrubbed up and go and assist Mr Kent. Mrs Goring is apparently a personal friend and he's promised to deliver her baby himself. It's quite unnecessary, of course, since we're not expecting any complications.'

Laura found Lucy already installed in the white-tiled delivery-room and a midwife had just finished assessing the situation: she had been listening to the foetal heart with an obstetrical stethoscope and she straightened up at the sight of Laura with a sigh of relief.

'Now you've come I'll get busy elsewhere. Mr Kent will be here as soon as he's got himself dressed up.'

She bustled out and Laura went up to the bed. She was not surprised that the patient failed to recognise her since she now looked totally different. Her smile was hidden behind her mask and only her eyes could convey the confidence which she hoped to instil into Lucy.

'How's it going?' she asked cheerfully.

'OK, I suppose, but I wish I could have something to help me to bear the pain. Surely I'm far enough advanced now?'

'I expect Mr Kent will let you have a few whiffs of Entodox when he comes in. He won't be long. In the meantime, try practising your breathing—it really does help.'

Martin entered at that moment, equally unrecognisable in his green cap and gown. His eyes no longer looked withdrawn and Laura thought she had never seen them so warm and smiling.

'I shall need to examine you, Lucy,' he said quietly, 'just to find out how far this impatient infant has managed to get in its headlong flight.'

He had beautiful hands, Laura thought in a detached sort of way; strong and well-shaped and very, very gentle. Hands that might have played a musical instrument if he had not gone in for medicine.

'It certainly won't be long now,' he was saying in an encouraging tone. 'Try not to push so hard. Your baby needs slowing up, not hurrying on.'

Since she had started her midwifery training two months ago Laura had seen innumerable babies born, yet it still thrilled her. When the baby girl, a fine seven-pounder, slid into view a short time later and almost immediately began a loud indignant cry, Laura shared fully in Lucy's delight. Gathering up the slippery little creature, she made sure the air passages were clear and then wrapped her in a towel and handed her to her mother, who received her with rapture.

'You've got what you wanted,' Martin said. 'A sister for your two boys.'

He was standing by the bed, looking down on mother and child, and there was something in his voice which caused Laura to glance at him curiously. He touched the baby's tiny hand and the little fingers immediately curled round his, but the mask hid all trace of facial expression and she couldn't guess at his feelings.

His voice cut sharply across her thoughts and she was glad that her own mask concealed the indignant flush which made her cheeks even hotter than they were already.

'It might be a good idea to stop daydreaming, Nurse, and get busy.'

'Yes, Mr Kent.' Her tone was quiet but inside she was seething. Some doctors could have made a remark like that and she would have taken it in good part, provided it had been said in the right way. Why did this man always seem to get under her skin?

As she held out her arms for the baby she said brightly, 'This little girl and I share a birthday, Mrs Goring, and it's a specially nice one, I think. March 21st is the first day of spring.'

'So it is.' Lucy pressed a kiss on the little dark head and handed the child over reluctantly. 'I hope that's a happy omen.'

Laura carried the tiny creature off to be washed

and dressed and while she was busy Sister put her head round the door. 'Everything all right, Nurse?' Receiving an affirmative reply, she went on, 'I hope you've got Mr Goring's phone number. His wife said she didn't want him to be told at present when she came in, but there's no reason for not ringing him now.'

'I'm sorry, Sister—I didn't think of it.'

'Then you should have done. I'll go and see her about it myself.'

Laura tied the ribbon of a minute vest and made sure the nappy was comfortable. In spite of Sister Leggett's disapproval she was glad she hadn't mentioned Mr Goring at the moment of his wife's happy triumph. With very little to go on, she had an uneasy feeling it wouldn't have been a welcome reminder.

No further reference was made to the matter, but Laura couldn't help noticing that Lucy had no visitors that evening. None, that is, at the normal visiting time, though she had one later.

Martin Kent slipped quietly into Cecilia Ward just before the night staff came on duty. It was very quiet then—even the babies were all asleep— and Lucy was resting in the corner bed which had been allotted to her in the first room. By chance, Laura was there when he arrived, saying good-night before leaving, an unnecessary but pleasant duty she usually tried to find time for.

She had her back turned when the consultant entered and the first she knew of his presence was when the patient exclaimed, 'Oh, you've brought my case, Martin! How kind of you. I'm longing to get into one of my own nighties.'

'I knew your mother wouldn't be able to leave the children.' He put it down on the locker. 'She sent her love and is thrilled to have a granddaughter this time. I expect she'll manage to come and see you some time tomorrow.'

On the point of leaving, Laura paused to take the case and unpack it. Consequently she couldn't avoid hearing the conversation which followed.

'Your mother wants to know whether you've decided on a name for the child,' Martin went on.

'I've been thinking—wouldn't it be rather nice to call her after the nurse? Specially as it's her birthday too. She was so kind to me, driving me here in her own car and all that. Turn round, Nurse, and tell us your name.'

Desperately embarrassed, Laura half turned, but there was no way she could avoid answering the question. 'It's Laura, but I really don't——'

Before she could finish the sentence Martin cut in on her. 'You always said you'd call the infant Lorraine if it turned out to be a girl. Personally I think you couldn't do better than that. It's a very pretty name.'

'Lorraine,' Lucy said thoughtfully. 'Yes, I must admit I do like it, and it's not so very different from Laura after all.'

'I think it's a *lovely* name,' Laura said fervently.

She put Lucy's nighties and toilet articles into

the locker and carried the case away, escaping from the room with relief. She hadn't wanted the baby to have her name because she believed it was an impulsive gesture on the mother's part, but she did think Martin needn't have shown so plainly how very much he disliked it. Shrugging off her annoyance, she unpacked a few articles of clothing for little Lorraine—if that was what she was to be called—and continued on her round.

Passing the nurses' station on her way to the locker-room, she sensed someone behind her and unwisely glanced over her shoulder, with the result that the consultant lengthened his stride and joined her.

'A word with you, Nurse,' he said curtly.

'Yes, Mr Kent?' Believing her conscience to be free, Laura waited impatiently.

'I understand that you drove Mrs Goring here in your car instead of calling an ambulance. Surely you must realise that you took a most unjustified risk? The child might have been born in the car which, I suppose, is probably a Mini or something nearly as small——'

'Actually, it's a Rover!' she flung back at him angrily.

'Really?' He was only momentarily taken aback. 'That hardly alters things, or are you so foolish as to imagine that you—a trainee midwife—could deliver a baby safely under such circumstances? The ambulancemen are trained to deal with all emergencies and one of them could have handled the birth while the other continued to drive to hospital.'

Laura tried to meet the hard glitter of his steel-grey eyes and failed, but she was determined to keep her end up.

'I'm very sorry if I made the wrong decision, Mr Kent, but I believe I acted for the best. It seemed to me of the utmost urgency that Mrs Goring should be got to hospital, and to send for an ambulance would have wasted valuable time.'

'Huh!' The stern lines of his angular face softened slightly. 'We'll say no more about it, Nurse, but kindly remember in future.'

Laura had the last word. 'I should think there's most unlikely to be a repetition,' she pointed out, and dived into the locker-room.

Quickly changing into the clothes she had worn for her birthday lunch, she struggled to put the annoying incident out of her mind. By the time she was ready to go down in the lift, she had nearly been successful.

Traffic still poured along the main road, though there were few pedestrians. As Laura waited at the crossing nearly opposite the Monk's Head—a pub which the hospital regarded as its own local—she again heard a voice behind her.

'Are you by any chance going to the Monk?'

The deep, slightly drawling tones were horribly familiar. She was well aware of the questioner's identity before she spun round and faced Martin Kent. 'Yes, I am. Why do you ask?'

'Because I'm going there too.' He grinned suddenly and his whole face changed. 'As you must know, Nurse—er—Marsden, I haven't been a consultant very long and the old habits die hard. I find I miss the convivial atmosphere of the Monk and occasionally indulge myself. Tonight I have the added excuse of drinking the health of Lucy's baby.' He paused and then added casually, 'Since it's your birthday as well, you might care to join me.'

For a moment Laura was too astonished to speak. Then she opened her mouth to tell him she was joining friends. But the brief silence had been fatal. He had, with what she considered his usual arrogance, taken her agreement for granted and, since the lights changed at that moment, had actually thrust his arm through hers and was steering her across the road.

Theoretically it was still possible for her to confess that she had a date, but somehow Laura felt ridiculously helpless. And as they walked along together her sense of humour began to assert itself as she pictured the faces of her two friends when she arrived with a man she was known to dislike so intensely.

She'd never live it down!

CHAPTER TWO

'CHEERS!' Martin's eyes met Laura's briefly across the top of his glass. They were unsmiling and her acknowledgement was equally cool. As she stood beside him near the bar, sipping her drink and talking about nothing very much, she continued to grapple with a feeling of unreality.

One quick look round the crowded Monk's Head had shown her that Jenny and Anita had not yet arrived. What was she to do when they turned up? How could she possibly excuse herself from her escort and join them without appearing abominably bad-mannered? It seemed an insoluble problem and she shelved it for the time being.

'By the way——' his tone was casual but Laura was nevertheless alerted to the fact that he was about to say something which mattered—'please don't mention Lucy Goring's husband to her. He won't be coming to visit because they've split up. There's going to be a divorce.'

She looked at him in surprise, thinking of the newborn baby already without a father. It seemed a strange time for husband and wife to part, unless. . . Jerking her mind from the path it was about to follow, she returned her attention to Martin.

'She told Sister,' he went on, 'and I'm letting you know so you won't keep on asking about her husband.'

So he'd invited her for a drink with no other motive than to warn her not to be tactless. 'I'm not a moron, you know,' Laura told him crossly. 'Anybody with a little sense could have detected that Lucy didn't want to talk about her husband.' She hesitated and then went rushing recklessly on. 'You didn't have to drag me over here to tell me that.'

For a moment Martin actually looked taken aback and then he said frostily, 'I don't know why you should jump to that conclusion.'

'It's obvious, isn't it?'

'That's a matter of opinion. But if it's what you want to believe then no doubt it appears obvious to you.'

She could think of no reply to that because she wasn't at all sure if it really was what she wanted to believe. They were silent for a moment and then he asked her if she would like another drink.

'No, thank you.'

Out of the corner of her eye she saw a surge of people at the door, and Jenny and Anita were swept in with them. There was no longer any problem about leaving Martin and joining them. After the recent disagreement he would doubtless be glad to get rid of her.

'I can see some friends of mine over there,' she said rapidly. 'Now that we've drunk the baby's health and—er—mine, I think I'd better join them. They'll be expecting me.'

'Very well,' he said carelessly.

Had she been rude after all? Laura glanced at him doubtfully, but he had already turned his back and she departed thankfully.

'So you got here first?' Jenny greeted her.

'It looks like it, doesn't it? What kept you?'

'We went to see a film this afternoon,' Anita said, 'and then we just pottered about, enjoying ourselves wasting time. How did you get on with the woman in labour?'

Laura grimaced. 'It was a bit traumatic actually, but gynaecologically things were OK. Sister disapproved of my turning up in ordinary clothes and Martin Kent was furious because I'd taken the risk of bringing Lucy Goring in my car instead of calling an ambulance. Apparently she's a great friend of his.'

'Interesting,' Jenny commented. 'What did she have?'

'A girl. Martin Kent delivered her and I assisted.'

'Bit unusual to have a consultant acting as a midwife! She must be a *very* great friend.' She pushed back her hair and stared curiously at Laura.

'What's Mr Goring like?' Anita asked.

'Your guess is as good as mine. We shan't be seeing him because they're getting a divorce.'

'But it's his child?'

'How on earth would I know that? Do you think I asked her?'

While Anita was admitting that it was a silly question, Laura suddenly noticed a vacant table. They dived for it and seated themselves in triumph. Around them the noise of the pub eddied and flowed. Doctors and nurses made up almost the entire clientele, and little groups talking shop filled up all the available space. Martin Kent, Laura noted, had disappeared.

They had switched from gin and tonic to orange juice when the outer door opened to admit a sandy-haired, freckled young man who wormed his way with some difficulty across to their table. His eyes were on Anita and he scarcely seemed to notice the other two.

'Hi!' she greeted him, her lovely eyes warm with affection. 'Have you been busy while I've been enjoying my day off?'

Gavin Forbes was house surgeon on the ward where she worked. Complete contrasts in appearance, they had been instantly attracted to each other.

'You could say so!' He grinned, neatly commandeered an unused stool and sat down. 'For your information, I'm dead on my feet. I shan't feel myself until I've got a couple of pints inside me.'

Laura stood up suddenly. 'Seeing as you're in such a bad way, Jenny and I will let you rest while we fetch you the first one.'

'What was that in aid of?' Jenny asked as they made their way to the bar.

'I thought they'd like to be on their own for a bit. They don't get much time together.'

As they joined a queue, Jenny looked back at the two heads, one black and the other reddish-fair. 'Do you think there's any future in that relationship?'

'I wouldn't like to say. Gavin's only doing his second six months as a house officer and it would be better all round if they didn't take themselves too seriously.'

'You can't always be sensible about that sort of thing.'

Laura inserted herself into a small gap and gave the order. 'It's not Gavin I'm worried about, but Anita's so warm-hearted and emotional. She could get hurt.'

'There's nothing we can do about it,' Jenny pointed out practically. 'Are you on early duty in the morning?'

'Yes, and I'd better not be late either.'

Cecilia Ward, when they reported for duty the next morning, was full to capacity.

'The population of Wickenfield is definitely going up,' Night Staff Nurse Ann Blake reported. 'You had two births yesterday and we had another two in the night. Four brand new babies to keep an eye on.'

'Are there any problems?' Laura asked.

'One is a thirty-week child and very small so he's in the Special Care Unit, but I think he'll be all right.'

She bent her head over the report she was writing and Laura went off to the babies' room to make the acquaintance of the new arrivals before going to see their mums.

When she reached Lucy Goring she found her radiant.

'I had a wonderful night and I feel marvellous this morning. I'm sure it's better to have a baby quickly—you don't get so exhausted. Martin doesn't agree with me, though. He says a birth should be much more controlled than Lorraine's was. We've definitely decided on that name, by the way.'

Did she mean she and Martin? Or had she consulted her family? For some reason Laura would have liked to have known the answer to that question, but it was impossible even to hint at her curiosity.

It was time to make preparations for serving breakfast, and after that the babies all had to be bathed and taken to their mothers for feeding, and then settled beside them for the day. Either Martin or his registrar usually did an informal round after that, and this morning it was the registrar who came. He was accompanied by the two housemen, who contrived to stay behind when he left and soon appeared in the kitchen.

'Just in time,' Jonathan said complacently,

observing Jenny and Laura unloading the patients' coffee trolley.

He was six feet three, and the tender care with which he handled a newborn baby was something which made even Sister feel a little sentimental. Nick was shorter and slightly plump, with a wispy brown beard which caused much derision among his friends.

'I don't know why you boys can't go to the canteen as we do,' Jenny said, spooning coffee into two mugs.

'Because we get it for free here.' Jonathan turned to Laura. 'Is it right you're going up in the world and moving into a house of your own?'

'Only because my aunt left it to me, and it's really a cottage.'

'Some people have all the luck.' Nick put two spoonfuls of sugar into his mug. 'Where is it? In Wickenfield?'

'No, just outside—a village called Mayes. Do you know it?'

Nick shook his head, and Jonathan said, 'I haven't had that pleasure but I shall hope to when you're in residence. You'll have a house-warming party, of course?'

Laura smiled. 'It depends on what my neighbours are like.'

Nick put down his mug with a thump. 'I knew the name rang a bell even though I've never been to the village myself. The boss lives there. You'll probably find you've got him as a neighbour!'

Her expression of dismay was so brief that nobody noticed it. 'My little place is in the middle of a row of cottages,' she said, 'so I don't think Mr Kent is likely to be a close neighbour.'

'His address is Hill House,' Jonathan put in. 'I've rather got the impression it's a biggish house with a large garden.' He swallowed the last of his coffee. 'Thanks a lot, girls; you've probably saved our lives.'

When the two young men had gone, Jenny glanced curiously at her friend. 'What's the matter?'

'Matter? Nothing.' Laura turned away to the sink and began to wash the used mugs. 'It's only that I just remembered something,' she went on with her back towards Jenny. 'Lucy Goring's address is Hill House, Mayes. Do you think they're living together?'

'*Really* living together or just sharing a house?'

'Might be either. But in view of the fact that she's getting a divorce—well, I can't help wondering.'

It was impossible to speculate further because Sister Leggett put her head in at that moment. She did not approve of housemen being given coffee in the kitchen, but regarded it as a necessary evil. Nurses gossiping when they should be working was another thing altogether.

'So there you are, Nurse Marsden,' she said to Laura. 'I would be obliged if you could spare the time to come and take the particulars of a new patient who's just arrived.'

Sarah Middleton was small, very young and very frightened. Her husband looked equally scared and Laura set herself to the task of making them both feel happier. It was a first baby and they seemed to have dashed off to the hospital soon after the pains began. They were lucky that Sister hadn't sent them home again to wait for a more advanced stage.

'When do you think the baby will be born?' Sarah asked nervously.

'It's difficult to say as early as this,' Laura told her. In her own mind she was fairly sure that the infant wouldn't put in an appearance until tomorrow but it wouldn't do to let the mother read her thoughts.

'Can my husband stay with me all the time?'

'Oh, yes, if that's what you want, but it would really be better if he went away as soon as you're comfortably settled and then came back later. You won't have to stay in bed, you know. You can go in the day-room and watch television. It will help to pass the time.'

The youthful father-to-be snatched eagerly at his reprieve and departed after a loving embrace. One of the midwives came in and examined Sarah, confirming Laura's opinion privately afterwards.

It was twenty-four hours before the Middleton baby slipped into the world, by which time his mother was exhausted. He was a fine child, giving no cause for alarm, but Sarah was so tired that she hardly seemed to have the strength to hold him.

'It was a forceps delivery,' the midwife told Laura, 'and she's got three stitches. She'll need to have a very quiet day.'

Things moved fast in the maternity block. That week several mothers, including Lucy Goring, went home and were replaced by others, and five more babies were born.

Bathing the last of these on Friday morning, Laura for the first time found it difficult to keep her mind on the red-skinned little creature in front of her. Normally bathing babies was a job she loved, but today her thoughts kept flying ahead to the evening when she was to move most of her possessions into her new home. She had found time during the week to choose the necessary items of furniture and hoped she would find that they had been delivered as promised. Tomorrow, if everything went according to plan, she would move in.

She was off duty at five o'clock and she went straight to her room in the nurses' home. It already looked forlorn, as though it belonged to no one. All the little personal items which had made it home had been packed—photographs of her family, the alabaster vase which was a souvenir of a holiday in Turkey, and the little white leather horse from Spain. Her cushions had been pushed into a big polythene bag and her pretty bedside light carefully packed in a box. Two big suitcases held all her clothes, and almost the only things remaining were what she would need for the night.

Jonathan had promised to help her transport all this to Lavender Cottage but she had not taken the offer very seriously. Housemen were not their own masters, and gynaecological ones were the most unreliable of all, due entirely to matters beyond their control. Laura was not at all surprised when he failed to turn up.

Sighing, she picked up the suitcases and began on the journey down to where her car waited to be loaded. It took her fifteen minutes to get everything transferred and packed in, and by the end of that time she was beginning seriously to wonder whether she could possibly be out of condition! The thought of having to unpack everything at the other end was making her feel quite depressed.

Depressed? What on earth was the matter with her? She ought to be feeling over the moon, and so she had been when she had first heard about her inheritance. So why had she changed, then?

Thinking it over as she drove along, Laura came to the conclusion that there was nothing the matter with her except an odd feeling of loneliness. She and Jenny and Anita had sometimes toyed with the idea of finding a flat and moving in together, but nothing had come of it. That would have been tremendous fun; quite different from this solitary journey to a new life.

By the time she reached Mayes she had talked

herself into a more suitable frame of mind. There
was her little cottage, snugly in the middle of a
row of five and with a lovely view across the
village green. Her aunt had been a keen gardener
and the minute front garden was bright with
daffodils and early tulips, which grew in such
abundance that the weeds were quite hidden. The
lavender hedge beside the path needed trimming,
though, and brushed against Laura's jeans as she
passed by.

Unlocking the door, she experienced a welcome
upsurge of excitement. This was her very own
place and she was going to be happy here; *of course*
she was.

The furniture had arrived and already looked
moderately at home. The carpets and curtains had
been Miss Marsden's and Laura intended to make
those do for a long time yet. The money she had
been left wouldn't stretch to new ones; she would
now have to budget for such unfamiliar items as
heating bills, poll tax, telephone and repairs,
which was intimidating to say the least.

Shrugging off such unpleasant thoughts, Laura
began to unload the car and soon the cottage
interior was looking rather like her room at the
nurses' home had done a short time earlier.

She had reached the last package, a huge paper
bag—she had run out of polythene—full of last-
minute items, when the calamity occurred. As she
heaved it out of the car boot, the bag split and a
miscellaneous assortment of rather shame-making

possessions fell on to the road and, in some cases, rolled about.

Laura used an expression which her aunt would certainly not have approved of, and quickly began to pick things up. She had retrieved her favourite mug from the middle of the road and was looking ruefully at its chips and cracks when she heard the sound of brakes being hurriedly applied. Spinning round, she saw a sleek BMW facing her.

'Good God!' Martin Kent got out hurriedly. 'It's Nurse Marsden! What the hell do you think you're doing?'

'Isn't it obvious?' Laura had been struck dumb with shock for a second, but she quickly recovered. 'I'm moving into this cottage.'

'Rather an unusual way of doing it,' he drawled. 'Couldn't you have found anything stronger than that paper bag?'

'Do you suppose I'd have used it if I had had anything better?' She swiftly bent to remove several paperback books from the path of his car and prayed that he would now depart.

'Looks like you could do with some help.' He drove on for a few yards so that the narrow road was no longer blocked, and parked neatly. To Laura's horror, he returned and began to salvage various items.

'I do wish you wouldn't bother——' she began furiously, and then subsided into silence as her fair skin grew scarlet with embarrassment.

Martin was holding a dingy, battered and one-eyed teddy-bear, and staring down at it curiously. 'A relic of childhood, I presume,' he suggested.

'Of course.' Laura tilted her chin defiantly. 'What else would it be?'

Ignoring the question, he handed it over with care. 'I managed to outgrow mine when I was about ten,' he volunteered. 'But boys are supposed to be tougher than girls. It's not true, of course. The more I see of women in childbirth, the more I admire them. Isn't there a well-known saying to the effect that the population of the world would come to an end if men had to produce the babies?'

Laura was in no mood for debate. She said a terse, 'I believe so,' and rapidly gathered up the things still lying in the road. Her arms full, she faced Martin Kent with determination. 'It was very kind of you to stop and help me but I can manage now. Goodbye.'

'If you try to carry all those, you'll only end up dropping them,' he observed. 'Let me take some.'

It was impossible to have an unseemly struggle right there. Already she had noticed someone peering out from behind a bank of geraniums next door, and so Laura reluctantly handed over half her load. Fuming, she led the way up the path and into the lobby.

'Nice little place,' Martin said, peering over her shoulder into the sitting-room. 'Are you going to live here by yourself?'

'Yes, I am—and I've got a lot to do getting it straight,' she added hastily.

'Want any help?'

'*No, thank you!*'

He grinned. 'Point taken.' But outside on the path he paused again. 'It doesn't look as though you're likely to get much of an evening meal. I'm sure Lucy would be delighted if you'd come and take pot luck at Hill House. She's always going on about how kind you were to her when she started labour at the Granville.'

Laura gasped, her thoughts whirling so that she felt almost dizzy. 'I was under the impression that you very much disapproved of my bringing her to the hospital in my car.'

'So I did—and still do. It's Lucy who's grateful, not me. How about it?'

Suddenly Laura was aware of hunger. She had had a very light lunch and done a lot of hard work since then, both before she came off duty and afterwards. There was a good deal to be done before she could even think of getting a meal at Lavender Cottage and the prospect of being provided with one without any effort on her part was very tempting.

'Are you *sure* Lucy won't mind?' she asked doubtfully.

'Of course I'm sure. As I said, she'll be delighted.' He looked critically at her dishevelled appearance. 'I'll give you two minutes to get ready.'

'OK.' Laura fled into the kitchen and, discovering a small mirror hanging near the sink, glanced into it apprehensively. Her normally smooth blonde hair was hanging over her eyes and there was a dirty mark on one cheek. Her hands, she discovered, were filthy. A vigorous wash in cold water and the rapid use of a comb restored her appearance somewhat and she hurried outside again.

Martin Kent was sitting in his car but he sprang out and opened the door for her. Used to the casual ways of housemen, Laura found this embarrassing, and she was horrified as she scrambled in to notice a hole in the knee of her jeans. She didn't match either the car or its owner's polished manners, and she hoped she wouldn't feel equally uncomfortable in Lucy's home.

Hill House also overlooked the village green, on the opposite side to Laura's cottage, and she could have walked the distance in two minutes. Nick's suggestion that Martin might turn out to be a neighbour flashed into her mind, as did her repudiation of it. Apart from actually living next door, you couldn't have anything much more neighbourly than sharing a village green.

'I had no idea it was so near,' she exclaimed. 'You needn't have bothered to wait for me.'

'You should watch that independence of yours,' he said curtly. 'You don't like people helping you to pick up things you've dropped, nor offering you an unexpected meal, and now you're objecting because I didn't leave you to walk. Are you always like this?'

She couldn't possibly tell him she didn't care for being helped by a man she disliked, so she merely shrugged and made no reply. During the few seconds that remained of the drive her mind flew back to their first meeting.

She had been a very new midwifery trainee and, although she had worked as a staff nurse on a medical ward for six months, in Cecilia she had felt like a student again. It was only her second day and she had been told to keep an eye on a young mother in the early stages of labour who was as nervous as Sarah Middleton.

'I've never been brave about bearing pain,' the patient gasped, clutching her back. 'They'll give me something for it, won't they?'

'Oh, yes,' Laura promised rashly. 'You won't be expected to suffer more than you can stand. They'll give you pethidine, I expect.'

'Can I have it now?'

'I'm afraid I'm not allowed to give you drugs without permission——'

She broke off and stood back as the door opened and a small group of people swept in—Martin Kent and his two house officers escorted by Sister. Ignoring her, they advanced on her charge and began to ask questions.

'I'm in terrible pain,' the patient moaned. 'The nurse says I can have something—pethidine, I think she called it—to help me to bear it. I need it *now*!'

Martin turned on his heel and glared at Laura. 'Did you say that?'

'I—I mentioned it but——'

He lowered his voice so that the words only just reached her. 'You had no right to say any such thing. It's much too soon for drugs, as you should know very well.'

She wanted to tell him she was new to midwifery but his steely glare had taken away all her normal courage and she merely murmured 'I'm sorry, Mr Kent,' and left it at that. He wouldn't have listened anyway, she felt sure.

That was two months ago, but the bad start in her relationship with the consultant had not been erased from her thoughts. She was wary of him even though she had ceased to be frightened.

Hill House stood well back from the road, with a sloping drive and a view right across the green to the church in the distance. It was Georgian in style, with a portico and tall windows on the ground floor. Martin parked his car to one side and ran up the two shallow steps to the porch, leaving Laura to follow more slowly. He flung open the front door and advanced into a tiled hall, calling out, 'Lucy! I've brought you a visitor.'

Hesitating behind him, Laura saw that it was not Lucy who appeared but someone who was presumably her mother. Introduced as Mrs Knighton, she was a small woman with short grey hair and wore cord trousers and a fawn silk shirt. She seemed slightly bemused on being presented with a guest for supper, but quickly rallied.

'My daughter's upstairs feeding the baby but I'm sure she'll be delighted to see you. Do come into the sitting-room and Martin will pour you a sherry.'

'I'll just run up and tell Lucy. Won't be a minute.'

He went up the elegant curving staircase two steps at a time and Laura stared after him. He seemed very much at home. Perhaps it *was* his house?

CHAPTER THREE

'LOVELY to see you again, Nurse.' Lucy came sailing into the large, comfortable sitting-room where her mother had deposited their guest.

She was wearing a loose blue dress and her mousy hair still hung lankly on either side of her face, but her large blue-grey eyes were bright and she looked happy. Martin came in behind her and went straight to the drinks table.

'Sweet or dry?' he asked, looking at Laura. 'The usual for you, Lucy?'

When they had been supplied, he poured himself a whisky and sat down. An odd little silence fell upon them.

'Martin says you're a neighbour of ours now,' Lucy said suddenly. 'Where actually do you live?'

'Lavender Cottage.' Managing to appear more at ease than she really felt, Laura began to talk about her new home. 'My aunt was the district nurse and she lived in Mayes nearly all her life. Perhaps you knew her?'

'Not really. I haven't been here long, you know. I only moved to the village about the time my marriage was going on the rocks. Martin had just been appointed a consultant at the hospital and it seemed a good idea.'

Totally unable to think of a suitable comment, Laura picked up her glass and gave her full attention to finishing the sherry. She was spared from further conversation by Mrs Knighton's putting her head in and announcing that supper was ready.

They ate in a small, cosy room referred to as the study. Although simple, the meal was delicious and Laura thoroughly enjoyed it in spite of the confusion in her mind.

'Do let me help with the washing-up,' she said, getting up from the table and beginning to collect the dishes.

Lucy's mother looked surprised. 'There's no need. I shall just put everything into the dishwasher and let it get on with it. You go and sit down and Martin will bring in the coffee.'

'Does it surprise you to see Martin so domesticated?' Lucy asked with a smile as they settled themselves.

'It does rather. I only know him as a consultant and he's—er—very different at the hospital.'

'I can imagine!' The smile faded and her eyes took on an inward look. 'My ex was a doctor and he never did a damn thing in the house. The two of them trained together and were friends for some years, but this business of the divorce has rather put paid to that.'

'Yes, I suppose it would,' Laura said vaguely.

Her curiosity thoroughly aroused, she longed to know more but at that moment Martin appeared with the coffee tray. He had just put it down on a small table when there came a wail from upstairs.

'Oh, dear,' Lucy said ruefully. 'I wish she'd waited a little longer.' She glanced at her guest with a slightly apologetic air. 'I'm afraid Lorraine thinks it's time for a meal and, as she's being fed on demand, I shall have to give in to her.'

'I'll fetch her,' Martin offered. 'You pour the coffee.'

He was soon back, carrying a bundle wrapped very untidily in a shawl. The baby was still dark haired, with a rosy face and wide open eyes. She was sucking her fingers, evidently in anticipation of having her hunger satisfied.

'Thanks.' Lucy took her baby from him and deftly arranged the shawl. Opening the bodice of her dress, she began to feed her with the greatest naturalness.

Laura had seen dozens of babies fed during her time in Cecilia. She had struggled with reluctant mothers and uninterested babies, and given good advice with as much authority as though she had been an experienced mother herself. Yet she found this intimate domestic scene embarrassing.

Glancing through the french windows at the end of the long room, she saw that the last of the daylight was rapidly fading. She had meant to do so much this evening and she had, so far, done precisely nothing. It would have been far better to stick to her intention of having a scratch meal when she had put away all the things she had brought from the nurses' home.

So why hadn't she done so?

With sudden resolution, she put down her coffee-cup and stood up. 'I really must be getting back to my cottage—there's such a lot to do. Thank you *very* much for the lovely meal.'

'You must come again, Laura.' Lucy gave her a warm smile and switched her gaze to Martin. 'You'll drive her back, won't you?'

Laura opened her mouth to protest but was forestalled.

'I shall do nothing of the sort. It's only a few hundred yards and Laura made it quite plain on the way here that she would have preferred to walk. I would hate to thwart her in her wish to walk home.'

He had spoken sharply, his expression deadpan, and Lucy seemed surprised. Not at all sure how to take his reply, Laura decided to ignore it.

'I'll be on my way, then.' She made a determined move towards the door. 'Thank you again.'

Martin caught her up by the front door and opened it for her. 'Enjoy your walk,' he said casually, and closed it again as soon as she was down the steps.

It was late when Laura got back to the hospital and she was too tired to feel sentimental about the last night in her familiar room. She got up early in the morning and, with a whole free weekend before her, was soon at Mayes with the last of her possessions and a firm intention to make Lavender Cottage into a home by the time she had to return to work on Monday. Everything went well and she had no problems that couldn't be solved fairly easily. By the time she went to bed on Sunday night, she felt very well satisfied with the way she had spent her time.

It was on Monday morning that things went wrong. The car wouldn't start.

Although she had had a driving licence since she was eighteen, Laura knew nothing about the mysterious interiors of cars; but this time it was clearly battery trouble and, apart from getting a kindly neighbour to start her with a jump lead, she knew it was hopeless.

A glance at her watch flung her into a panic and she began walking as fast as she could in the hope of thumbing a lift. Surely, at such an early hour and with so many commuters driving into Wickenfield, it would be quite safe?

She hadn't noticed that rain was threatening and, as she reached the main road, it began in earnest. Turning up the collar of her navy raincoat, she plodded on, glancing over her shoulder frequently in the hope of seeing a car slow down. For a while nothing happened and she was beginning to despair when she heard the unmistakable sound she had been waiting for.

'Hop in!' said a familiar voice. 'Unless, of course, you'd rather keep on walking?'

Martin Kent, of course. It would have to be him just when she really needed a lift and would look ridiculous if she refused.

Her fractional hesitation did not escape him and he said curtly, 'Don't stand there dithering. I've been sent for to cope with an emergency.'

With a murmured, 'Thank you,' Laura got in and shut the door. Almost before it had closed they were racing down the road. She waited until they were obliged to halt at the traffic lights on the outskirts of Wickenfield and then, her professional curiosity getting the better of her, enquired as to the nature of the emergency.

'Urgent Caesarean. It was expected to be a normal birth but the baby is showing signs of distress. It's Tom's free weekend,' he added, referring to his registrar, 'and so they sent for me. Where's your own car?'

'Flat battery.'

'Hadn't you realised it was about to pack up?'

'I've been too busy thinking about other things.'

'Even so, I should hardly have thought it would be possible to miss anything so obvious.'

She let him have the last word and a moment later they reached the hospital. Up in Cecilia Ward she found that the emergency case had been prepared for operation and the normal work of the ward was in progress. For a while she was too busy to ask questions, but eventually she encountered Jenny in the kitchen and paused to find out more about the patient who was having a Caesarean.

'Mrs Simpson came in yesterday afternoon. She's forty-two and this is her first baby so you can guess how important it is.'

'Is the baby's condition really serious?'

'Could be, but I hope not. Luckily Martin Kent got here very quickly. He's in theatre now so no time's been wasted.'

Sister came in just then and they separated hastily. There was still plenty to do and, when the rush wasn't too great, Laura enjoyed this part of the day. She loved handling the babies and taking them to their mothers. Some of them needed a lot of encouragement to feed, and the mothers were sometimes nervous about their ability to supply enough nourishment.

'I'm sure I shall never manage it when I'm on my own,' Sarah Middleton wailed. 'There'll be so much to do and I shan't have time for these long drawn-out feeds.'

'You'll have to tell yourself that nothing is so important as giving your baby his food. Never mind about the house—just let things go until you and the baby are properly organised,' Laura said cheerfully.

'It's easy for you to talk! My husband won't at all appreciate being neglected.'

'There's no reason why you should neglect him. You'll have time for both baby and his father— you'll see.'

But Sarah would not let herself be convinced and in her heart Laura did not really blame her. Nobody who hadn't experienced motherhood could possibly know what it was like, but you had to pretend or new mothers would be even more nervous than some of them were already. Sarah, for instance, was worrying about almost everything and the happiness and excitement of becoming a mother had vanished.

'She mustn't be allowed to develop postnatal depression,' Sister said firmly. 'I rely on you nurses to do your utmost to keep her courage up.'

When Laura had done all she could for the Middleton baby and his mother, she went to help the mother of the premature infant to express her milk so that the child could be fed without being removed from the incubator.

'Time for your coffee break, Nurse.' Sister had appeared in the nursery as Laura was removing her mask after attending to the tiny creature.

She took off her plastic apron and set off for the canteen, which was some distance from the maternity block and reached by a covered way. She had collected her coffee and a chocolate biscuit, and even found an unoccupied small table, when she heard a voice behind her.

'Mind if I join you?'

It was Martin, his normally smooth hair on end after he had dragged off the theatre cap. In addition to his coffee he was carrying a plate laden with a large toasted sandwich.

'It's a free country,' Laura said, softening the words with a rather forced smile. 'Are you going to eat all that?'

'I certainly didn't buy it just to sit and look at it.' He took a large bite and continued a little indistinctly, 'For your information, I had no breakfast this morning.'

'How did the Caesarean go?'

'It was a routine case as far as the operation was concerned.' He frowned, seemed about to add something and then changed his mind.

'I suppose Mrs Simpson will be back in the ward soon?'

'Oh, yes. In some ways having your baby delivered by Caesarean is less traumatic than labour.'

'Surely that only applies when an operation is intended from the beginning? This patient had already been in labour for some time,' Laura protested.

Martin stared at her across the table. 'What an argumentative girl you are! Don't you ever accept a statement without challenging it?'

'Of course I do.' Laura flushed indignantly. She wanted to add that some people made her want to argue more than others, but thought better of it. Martin continued to devour his sandwich while studying her thoughtfully, as though weighing up the matter of her argumentative nature. His scrutiny was embarrassing, and, to take her mind off it, Laura struggled to keep the conversation going.

'I'm thinking of getting rid of my aunt's old car and buying something smaller and a bit more up to date.'

Pleased with his immediate interest, she congratulated herself on thinking of something which could be guaranteed to catch the attention of almost any male. At the end of her coffee break she went back to the ward with her head buzzing with advice.

It was all a bit academic actually, she reminded herself as she put on her cap in the locker-room. The most pressing need was a new battery for the old Rover.

Considerably to her surprise, the same thought seemed to have occurred to Martin. He came up to the ward during the afternoon and detained her for a moment near the nurses' station.

'What are you doing about that flat battery?'

'I haven't done anything so far but——'

'If you can get yourself back to Mayes when you go off duty, I'll come along with a jump lead and start it for you. Then you can drive to that garage on the Wickenfield bypass that's open late and get a new battery fitted. OK?'

'I couldn't possibly put you to so much trouble!' she exclaimed.

'Won't take much more than five minutes.' And he added explosively, 'For heaven's sake, don't start arguing about it!'

That silenced her vocal chords but did nothing to still the turbulence in her mind. It almost seemed as though this man she so much disliked

was going out of his way to put her in his debt and
she could think of no reason why he should be
taking the trouble.

The arrival of Mrs Simpson and her baby gave
her something else to think about. Both were
asleep and did not wake when transferred to bed
and cot. The mother's condition gave no cause for
alarm but the tiny girl had a bluish tinge which
Sister viewed with concern.

'You think she's suffering from taking too long
over her birth?' Laura ventured to ask.

'Certainly not, Nurse Marsden.' Sister's red nose
seemed to glow with indignation. 'I'm surprised
you should make such a suggestion. Are you
intending to imply there was carelessness of some
sort?'

Laura was considerably taken aback and hurried
to deny it. 'I wouldn't dream of suggesting that,
Sister.'

'I should hope not. I have the assurance of the
Night Staff Nurse that the Caesarean was per-
formed without delay.' Her expression changed
and she went on in a worried tone, 'What I had in
mind was the possibility of some congenital heart
defect. Perhaps what is commonly known as a
hole in the heart.'

'Poor little thing!' Laura exclaimed.

'You mustn't take it for granted that I am right.
Even someone with my experience can make an
occasional mistake. We must see what Mr Kent

says. And in the meantime, not a word to the mother. Have I made that quite clear?'

'Yes, Sister, but if Mrs Simpson asks why the baby is such a bad colour, what shall I say?'

'It's part of your job to think of something suitable, Nurse, and I'm sure you'll manage very well. Do you happen to know if Mr Kent is still in the ward?'

'I think he went to see someone in the end room.'

'I'll waylay him and ask him to take a look at Baby Simpson.' On the verge of bustling off, Sister added, 'We really are very fortunate in our consultant. I've never known anyone make himself so readily available. There is a very shocking tendency nowadays to pay more attention to the private patients than to those who come under the NHS, but Mr Kent isn't like that.'

Laura had to admit that she was right, but the more other people praised the man the more determined she seemed to become not to fall under his spell. And as for getting neighbourly with him in the village, she had quite made up her mind that once he had started her car for her she would avoid any future contact outside the hospital.

Although Laura was present, she kept very much in the background when he came to see the Caesarean baby.

'I agree with your diagnosis,' he told Sister. 'I suspected it down in theatre but there was no immediate danger to the child and so I said nothing. We'll wait until she's a bit older before any remedial action is taken, but the mother must be told, of course.'

'Her husband will be here this evening,' Sister remembered. 'He's been away on a business trip and couldn't get back any quicker.'

'If Mrs Simpson is well enough—and I think she will be—I'll tell them both then.' His eye suddenly alighted on Laura. 'You must be extremely careful, Nurse, not to let her guess she has any cause for concern.'

'I've already told Nurse Marsden that,' Sister interposed crossly, 'and, in any case, my nurses aren't in the habit of being indiscreet, Mr Kent.'

He raised his eyebrows fractionally but made no comment and left the ward. Pleased that she was apparently considered more trustworthy than had appeared to be the case, Laura set herself to the task of thinking out various ways of parrying awkward questions should the need arise.

But, as so often happened when she had prepared herself for difficulties, when she eventually carried the Simpson baby to her mother Mrs Simpson did not even notice the hint of bluishness. She was delighted that her child did not have the usual raw red look.

'Isn't she pretty, Nurse?' she exclaimed. 'So feminine with that clear pale skin and fine soft hair. I think she's absolutely sweet, don't you?'

'I think all babies are sweet,' Laura said with perfect truth, 'but some are sweeter than others.'

She smiled as she spoke, not at all surprised that Mrs Simpson obviously took it for granted that her own infant was among the latter.

She was not present when Martin broke the news about a possible hole in the heart but he told her about it when he turned up to start her car later on.

'They took it very well but I'm afraid it was a shock to them, particularly as this is their first child.'

'It's such a shame!' Laura burst out. 'Why do these things happen?'

He straightened up from fixing the leads to the Rover's battery. 'You tell me,' he said soberly.

'I wish I could.'

For the moment she had forgotten he was a consultant whom, for some reason, she didn't very much like, and was talking to him as though he were a friend. She was reminded of their true relationship when he said in what seemed to her to be a dictatorial tone, 'Off you go now and see about that new battery, and whatever you do don't stall the engine until the old one's had time to build up a little.'

'I hope I shan't stall it at all,' she said frostily, adding with an effort, 'Thank you so much for helping me, Mr Kent. I'm very grateful.'

'You can reward me by ceasing to be so bloody formal,' he flung back at her. 'We're neighbours now—remember? In future I'd be obliged if you'd call me Martin when we're not at the hospital. You don't call Lucy "Mrs Goring", so why should I be different?'

Laura could think of several reasons, but she merely answered coolly, 'Very well—Martin. I'll try and remember.'

For the remainder of that first week at Lavender Cottage Laura had no obligation whatsoever to call the gynaecological consultant by his forename, a state of affairs which gave her considerable satisfaction. It was a happy week. She spent the first part of it working hard to make her inheritance feel like home. She arranged her scanty furniture to the best advantage, and, with the cushions and ornaments she already possessed scattered about, it really did begin to look attractive. At the end of the week she invited Jenny and Anita to supper and took pleasure in serving them a meal which had not come from the supermarket deep-freeze.

When they had finished their meal they washed up quickly and then sat for some time over their coffee, after which Laura drove them back to the hospital. The cottage seemed very quiet when she returned to it—quiet and rather empty—and she went straight to bed.

She and Jenny were both on early duty in the morning. There were no babies expected and, after the usual rush was over, the ward was comparatively peaceful. As a result they were lucky enough to be sent off for their coffee break together.

Afterwards they even managed to snatch a few minutes out in the grounds.

The chestnut trees, which were all that remained of the original hospital garden, were shaking out their new leaves and there were tulips instead of daffodils in the beds. The two girls sat down on a seat and lifted their faces to the sun.

'I can't believe it's April already,' Jenny said dreamily. 'We'll soon be looking forward to our summer holidays.'

'I probably shan't be able to afford one this year.' Laura spoke absently, her mind elsewhere, and after a moment she revealed the trend of her thoughts. 'Do you think Gavin and Anita are serious?'

Jenny gave the question her full consideration. 'I think *she* may be, and that means I hope Gavin feels the same. But he's at the beginning of his career and it's more than likely he won't want to tie himself down too quickly.'

'Since when did that stop anybody falling in love?'

'I was only trying to look at it from a sensible point of view. Anyway, what you and I think about it isn't going to make the slightest difference.'

'I wouldn't want Anita to get hurt,' Laura said thoughtfully. 'She's so very vulnerable.'

'I know.' Suddenly Jenny gave a shriek of horror. 'Have you seen the time? Come *on*, for goodness' sake!'

Well aware that Sister Leggett believed in old-fashioned discipline, they expected to be scolded for being late but she scarcely seemed to notice. She was unnaturally quiet today, Laura reflected, and wondered, not for the first time, if she wasn't feeling well.

It was time for the babies to be fed again. Although feeding on demand was theoretically encouraged, it was not altogether practicable in hospital and some sort of routine was adhered to if possible. Counting the premature baby, whose mother had been discharged, there were only five of them. Sarah Middleton had gone home, a little more convinced than she had been earlier that she would be able to cope, but the health visitor had been alerted as to her mental condition and would keep in close touch.

Mrs Simpson was still there but would be leaving on Sunday. Her little girl looked rather better even though it now seemed certain that the tiny heart was malformed and there would have to be an operation when she was old enough.

'Poor little mite,' the mother said when Laura brought the infant to her. 'It does seem a shame that she should have to be messed about by surgeons at her age.'

Laura agreed heartily though she did not say so. She always felt desperately sorry for parents having to face up to something like this. It was different for the nurses. They saw and handled so many babies that they could at least sometimes forget about particular problems, but to the parents their baby was the only one in the world.

'Babies are incredibly tough,' she reminded Mrs Simpson, 'and they can stand a very great deal. You mustn't worry about it. Just leave it to the experts.'

'That's what Mr Kent said. He *is* nice, isn't he, Nurse? My husband and I like him so much.' Laura smiled but made no comment, and the patient went on speaking. 'The nurses are all nice too and it makes such a difference. In a way I'm quite enjoying my stay in hospital.'

Her words made pleasant hearing and Laura stored them away in her mind, to be remembered perhaps when they had to put up with a different kind of patient—somebody who seemed to have a grudge against all the nursing staff and constantly complained of neglect.

Luckily these were rare, but they had one the following morning.

CHAPTER FOUR

Mrs Denby was an unnatural blonde with a thin mouth which looked as though it had never learnt to smile. She arrived before the nurses had finished bathing babies, and was highly indignant when she was told to go home and return when the pains were stronger.

'You live very close to the hospital,' the midwife in charge said reasonably, 'and it will be better for you to be in your own home doing your usual Sunday jobs. The time won't seem nearly so long if you keep yourself occupied.'

The pencilled eyebrows rose in astonishment. 'But I'm in no condition to *work*!'

'Of course she's not,' put in Mr Denby gallantly. He was a small man and had a harassed look.

But the midwife was firm and they were obliged to leave the ward. Laura, who had overheard some of the conversation, made a rueful grimace. 'I'm not looking forward to seeing *her* again,' she told the midwife.

'Nor me. She's the sort who demands painkillers long before she needs them and expects us to dance attendance all the time.'

'Is her husband going to be present?'

'No—the lucky man! She said quite frankly she

didn't want him and I think he was glad to escape.'
The middle-aged midwife, who had seen so many
births, rubbed her chin thoughtfully. 'It's extraordinary how people vary, but at least very few
are as difficult as Mrs Denby is likely to be.'

The afternoon was peaceful, with a cheerful
hum of visitors and no alarms, but when Laura
returned from a late tea break she found Mrs
Denby installed in the labour-room and behaving
exactly as the midwife had predicted. None of
them allowed her to ruffle them. She received the
same treatment as anyone else would have done
and hers was the only temper on public view.

'Looks like we're going to be short-staffed,'
Jenny said, appearing suddenly at the nurses'
station. 'Vicky Walker's with Mrs Denby at the
moment, but she's got one of her migraines
coming on and wants to go off early before it gets
bad. That means we're going to be extra busy after
the visitors have gone.'

'You wanted to get away punctually, didn't
you?'

Jenny nodded. 'I promised to pop in and see the
family for a short time. How about you?'

'I'm in no particular hurry. Is Mrs Denby pro-
gressing OK?'

'Oh, yes—the contractions have speeded up a
lot.'

They separated as the midwife approached but
Laura found herself called back.

'I shall want you to join me as soon as Mrs

Denby is moved to the delivery-room.' She added the information about Nurse Walker's migraine. 'You can deliver the baby provided there are no complications, and if you could stay on a bit— should it turn out to be necessary—it would be very useful. I doubt if this baby will be born before eight o'clock or even later, and I don't want to involve the night staff at this stage.'

Hours were apt to be elastic in Cecilia Ward and Laura made no complaint. 'You were quite right about being short-staffed,' she said to Jenny later when they met in the nursery, each burdened with a tiny red-faced infant. 'I've been asked to help with Mrs Denby.'

Jenny put her baby down and changed its nappy with practised ease. 'Perhaps I ought to cancel my visit——'

'No, of course not. I don't mind a bit. If I'm lucky, I'll be allowed to deliver the Denby infant.'

'D'you know something, Laura? I believe that woman is absolutely terrified of pain. She's forgotten all her antenatal training—if she ever had any—and consequently she gets herself into such a state of nervous tension with every contraction that she makes it all so much worse for herself, and doesn't help the baby either.'

'She's having pethidine, isn't she? That ought to relax her.'

'She's been complaining it isn't enough and asking for an epidural.'

'At this stage?'

They both smiled and continued with their work. When it was all finished Laura went to offer her services in the labour-room.

She had expected to find Mrs Denby about to be moved but she seemed to be dozing and the midwife was studying her watch with frowning intensity. Eventually she looked up and beckoned Laura over to the window. 'I'm not too happy about the way things are going,' she murmured. 'It's ten minutes since she had a contraction and that's all wrong.'

'I thought she'd been getting on quite well.'

'So she was, but just recently everything slowed down. It happens sometimes and it's never a good sign.' She hesitated, glancing at the woman in the bed. 'Mr Kent's on call this weekend and I think, just to be on the safe side, we'll ask him to come and give his opinion. We daren't take any chances, so will you go and phone him, please?'

Laura sped away at once, looked up the number and dialled. Almost immediately she heard his deep, slightly drawling voice. 'Martin Kent here.' It took only a moment to relay the message and he asked for no details. It was sufficient for him that an experienced midwife considered his presence necessary. 'I'll be there in ten minutes,' he said promptly.

While they waited for him Mrs Denby had a contraction. As Laura took her groping hand in a firm clasp she was unhappily aware that this was a very minor pain indeed.

'It's easier now,' Mrs Denby gasped. 'Does that mean the baby's nearly here?'

Glad that she didn't have to answer that question, Laura waited for what the midwife would say.

'It means that we're not letting you suffer too much, my dear. In fact, we've decided to give you extra help and one of the doctors will be here in a few minutes.'

'I can't think why I didn't have a doctor ages before this. Perhaps it wouldn't have taken so long then.'

'First babies are nearly always slow. Your labour hasn't been at all prolonged.'

Fortunately the door opened just then and Martin came in. He had Jonathan with him and Mrs Denby opened her eyes again.

'Two doctors,' she said complacently. 'It'll soon be over now.'

'How much is she dilated?' Martin asked the midwife in a quiet tone, and on receiving the reply, 'Two fingers,' he frowned, considered for a moment and then turned his attention to Laura. 'I shall need forceps, Nurse—quickly, please.'

When she returned he was preparing to administer the longed-for spinal injection, and Mrs Denby seemed to have forgotten her weariness now that she was receiving the attention she considered her due. Disappointed that she had lost the chance of delivering the baby, Laura joined Jonathan in the background where he was trying to keep out of the way, since he was there on this occasion only as an observer.

Without any proper contractions to help, the procedure of assisting the Denby baby into the world was slow and difficult. With immense patience, Martin bent to his task, talking encouragingly to the mother as he worked. They could see the top of the head now and Laura found herself holding her breath as the forceps drew it gently and with infinite patience further into view.

At her side Jonathan's eyes twinkled over his mask. 'I can almost feel it myself,' he whispered.

She did not return the twinkle. Perhaps he didn't yet know how serious the situation was or he wouldn't have joked—at least she hoped not. And then she remembered that housemen needed to see the funny side of things sometimes or their lives would be insupportable, and she forgave him his ill-timed humour.

Suddenly there was an exclamation from the midwife. 'You've got a little son, Mrs Denby!'

Martin was holding the child up by his heels. He delivered a sharp slap to his back but no loud indignant cry resulted. The small heart would need a more powerful stimulant than that if it was to begin its work.

Every minute was precious if lack of oxygen was not to cause irreparable brain damage. While the midwife attended to the mother, who seemed quite unaware of danger, Martin carried the infant into the adjoining room, followed closely by Laura.

Together they worked over the little body as he tried everything he knew to get the baby to draw his first breath.

And suddenly it happened. There was a gurgling gasp as the small chest inflated, and then a feeble cry which rapidly increased in volume. It seemed like a miracle and Jonathan came forward to share in the rejoicing. Finding them still grave-faced, he looked questioningly at his boss.

'He's OK, isn't he? You were quick enough?'

Martin turned to Laura. 'You took a note of the time of birth?'

'Yes, and I checked again when the baby cried.'

'Well?' he demanded impatiently as she paused for a calculation.

'Three minutes and forty-five seconds exactly.'

Martin drew a long breath of relief and smiled. 'So we just made it!' His gloved hand touched hers briefly and withdrew. 'I had almost begun to fear we might not.'

'Why didn't the labour proceed normally?' Jonathan demanded. 'She was all right until the end of the second stage, wasn't she? So why did things slow up like that?'

Martin shrugged. 'These things happen occasionally and we don't always know the reason. If you're going in for gynaecology, Jonathan, you'll have to accept that nature doesn't always keep to the rules.'

While they had been talking Laura had been busy preparing the baby for presentation to his mother. It was a moment which never failed to give her pleasure. Fortunately Mrs Denby did not seem to know that it was customary to give a new baby immediately to the mother to hold, and therefore did not complain at the delay. But she took him gingerly and immediately commented on his small size.

'How much does he weigh, Nurse?'

'I haven't put him on the scales yet.'

'I thought that was what you were doing.' Her sharp face softened as she looked down at the wrinkled little creature. 'He isn't like either of us, but I suppose it's too soon to tell.'

'You had better go and tell Mr Denby to come and see his wife and child,' the midwife told Laura. 'He's had a long spell in the waiting-room.'

She pulled off her mask as she went, realising suddenly how tired she was. When she had congratulated him and conducted him to the delivery-room, Laura made sure she was not required any more and trailed wearily off towards the locker-room.

'You still here?' Ann Blake, the night staff nurse, asked as she passed the nurses' station. 'Been doing overtime?'

'I got involved early this evening and stayed on, but I'm going home now.'

'I should think so. Had you noticed it's ten o'clock?'

Laura hadn't. Time had ceased to mean much—

except for those terrible minutes in the annexe to the delivery room.

She changed out of uniform and put on the skirt and sweater she had worn that morning. Her face stared back at her from the mirror, big-eyed and pale, her hair still flattened by the close-fitting operation cap. She looked terrible!

Luckily no one was likely to see her, she thought. But she was wrong about that.

She was walking wearily to the hospital car park, taking deep breaths of the fresh night air but not feeling much better for it, when footsteps rapidly overtook her and Martin appeared at her side.

'You're walking like you hardly know how to put one foot in front of the other,' he commented. 'Will you bite my head off if I suggest you leave your car here overnight and let me give you a lift home?'

'I don't feel disposed to bite anyone's head off at the moment,' she confessed with a wan smile, 'but I can't accept your offer because I shall need my car in the morning.'

'Are you on early?'

'N-no, not till two o'clock, but I shall still need the car.'

Convinced that she had settled the matter, Laura got into her car and drove slowly and with some-what exaggerated care out into the main road. As she turned towards Mayes she was vaguely aware of lights behind her but thought nothing of it, and it wasn't until she drew up in front of her cottage that she realised that she had a follower. Martin was stopping too.

What on earth could he possibly want now? Distinctly cross, and yet with strangely throbbing pulses, she paused and looked back.

He wound down the window. 'After an evening like we've just had, there's nothing to beat a run out into the country—or even to the sea. It's wonderful for helping you to unwind. Will you come?'

'But aren't you on call?'

'Not now.' He got out and stood looking down at her, his face pale in the starlight and his eyes glinting almost as though he were smiling. 'It'll do us both good,' he urged, 'so stop dithering and do something rash for once.'

'What do you mean?' she demanded.

'You really want to know?'

'Yes, I do!'

'All right, then, you've asked for it. I think you like your life all nice and tidy, which means you hardly ever do anything crazy, such as going off for a drive in the middle of the night——'

'It's barely half-past ten,' she interrupted. 'That's not the middle of the night.'

'Figure of speech.' He put his hands on her shoulders and gave her a little shake. 'Come on, Laura—be a devil for once!'

After that it was impossible to refuse, but Laura was seething as she got into the BMW. How dared Martin analyse her character like that? He'd got it all wrong anyway—or had he? She'd certainly never done anything as mad as this—or not since her carefree teenage days.

'If you don't mind,' she said deliberately, 'I'd like to go as far as the sea.'

'Great!' He gave her an approving pat. 'With any luck the moon will be up by the time we get there.'

How far was it? Laura wasn't sure and didn't care anyway. She opened the window a crack and felt the revitalising effect of a cool draught on her flushed face. Leaning back in the comfortable seat, she gave herself up to the pleasure of being driven in a fast car by a man who handled it with the utmost ease. Only one small worry remained at the back of her mind and occasionally gave her a prod.

What would Lucy think of this? How much would she mind?

The miles slipped by, unpunctuated by conversation. They crossed a stretch of heathland and went through several villages, coming eventually to a small town which Laura recognised as Sheerton-on-Sea. But Martin did not drive straight to the sea through the main street; instead, he went round the outskirts and reached a deserted road which followed the coast. An empty car park lay before them and he drove to the far end from which they had an uninterrupted view of the tossing North Sea. When he switched off the engine, the sound of the waves filled the silence with its soft swishing noise.

'Will this do?' he asked.

Laura sat up and drew a long breath of pleasure. 'It's so lovely—so unutterably peaceful!'

And at that moment, the moon swam out from behind some clouds and flung a silver path across the water.

'Dead on cue!' Martin laughed and slipped his arm along the back of the seat. 'Feeling better?'

Laura gave a long sigh. 'Yes, thank you.'

Her head seemed to have found a resting place against his shoulder and it felt very comfortable there. When he leaned his cheek against her hair she accepted it as perfectly natural. In an easy companionable silence they enjoyed the beauty of the night and the quietness of their surroundings after the tension of the day.

But after a while a subtle change crept in and Laura was suddenly aware of tension of a completely different kind. Martin stirred, his other arm came round her and she was held pinioned to her seat. She could feel his heart beating strongly through his sweater and knew with absolute certainty that he was going to kiss her.

Did she want him to? A short time ago Laura would have answered that question with a vigorous denial. Now she wasn't sure. It didn't look as though she would be consulted anyway. His lips were fiercely demanding and at first she surrendered to them, lying quiescent in his arms and allowing her senses to banish conscious thought.

How long it lasted she didn't know. Perhaps only a few seconds. But suddenly Laura began to fight. She *didn't* want Martin to kiss her like that, or in any other way either. Maybe it was naïve of her, but she hadn't realised that all he had wanted was a necking session. She had listened to all that rubbish about her life being too orderly and the need for doing something mad, and she had allowed it to influence her to an absurd degree.

But she was back in her right mind now.

With an effort she wrenched her head sideways, at the same time pushing with both hands against his chest. 'Let me alone! I don't like being—being mauled.'

She could sense his astonishment but his recovery was speedy. He was at once angry and icily cold. 'I don't care much for your choice of words. I'm not in the habit of *mauling* women. And as for pretending you don't like being kissed, that's a load of rot.'

Aware of how much she had at first responded to his demands, and how fiercely his virility had aroused her own sexual feelings, Laura was temporarily bereft of words. But she quickly rallied. 'I was taken by surprise. I didn't have time to protest.'

'And you didn't want to either. I just don't believe it was entirely because I surprised you.'

There was nothing she could answer to that and she took refuge in a rather forlorn, 'Please, won't you drive me home?'

'With pleasure!' he said bitterly.

They did not speak on the homeward journey. When she got out of the car outside Lavender Cottage, Laura was uncertain whether to thank him or not. In view of what had happened it seemed a bit ridiculous. Eventually she decided to be frank.

'If you really did take me for a drive to help me unwind, then I'm grateful. I'm not nearly so tired now as when I left the hospital.'

'That's something, anyway,' he said curtly. 'I'm glad the expedition wasn't entirely wasted.' He hesitated and then added, 'You may not believe me, but my intentions actually were as you've just stated. What happened later was incidental and certainly doesn't warrant all the fuss you've been making. Goodnight.'

Feeling thoroughly snubbed and not liking it at all, Laura fled indoors, made herself a hot drink and went to bed.

But sleep did not come easily. Over and over again she relived the 'incident' by the sea. There was no doubt in her mind now that she really had made an absurd fuss and, looking at it with hindsight, she would have given anything to have behaved in a more mature way. If it had been any other man—Jonathan, for instance—she would have looked on it as a light-hearted interlude, of no importance whatsoever.

Why couldn't she have felt like that with Martin?

She fell asleep at last and slept late. When she

woke after nine, the telephone was ringing—it was Anita.

'I remembered you said you were off this morning and I am too, so can I come over?'

'Yes, of course, but how will you——?'

'I can borrow a bicycle. See you!'

Laura ate a quick breakfast and had just finished tidying the kitchen when her visitor arrived. She had bought a few items since her two friends had come to supper and now she offered a tour of inspection before producing coffee.

They carried their mugs out into the tiny garden, and sat talking in the sun on a dilapidated seat. Anita stayed to lunch—a scratch meal of bread and cheese and fruit—and then they set off by car and bicycle so as to be in good time for duty at two o'clock.

Laura was soon summoned to attend to the admission of a new patient. Mrs Jennings was having her third baby and knew exactly what was expected of her. She had timed her contractions carefully and knew the interval between them almost to the second. She took it for granted that she would have to provide a specimen of urine and undressed without being told. When Laura produced the sphygmomanometer and took her blood pressure, she enquired what it was and appeared to understand its significance. Obviously a model patient! Smiling to herself, Laura hoped that the baby would keep to the rules too.

Sister Leggett was clearly assuming that it would

for she told Laura she could deliver the child if it
looked like arriving before she went off duty. 'I
think it probably will, Nurse,' she said. 'I remember Mrs Jennings quite well and she was quick
with her second child. I presume you wouldn't
mind staying on for a while if the birth is imminent
when you're due to go off? I don't approve of
mothers having to put up with a change of midwife unless it's necessary.'

Agreeing at once, Laura was reminded of the
previous evening when she had stayed on for
some time. Since Sister had been off duty, she
probably didn't know about that.

Was it *really* only yesterday that she had driven
to the sea with Martin? She hadn't seen him all
day and for that she was grateful. She had a
horrible feeling that she would find their next
meeting embarrassing.

Yet when it happened it seemed so ordinary that
she wondered why she had been apprehensive.
He came into the delivery-room just as she had
brought the Jennings baby into the world in
triumph and was about to present him to his
mother. Exactly what he was doing there she
couldn't imagine, unless Sister had told him one
of the trainee midwives was in charge and he had
looked in to check that everything was all right. It
wasn't necessary because there was an experienced midwife handy in case anything went
wrong.

Whatever the reason, he was there, and after a

moment when her pulses raced Laura faced him calmly, secure behind her mask.

'Everything OK?' he asked quietly. And when she said demurely, 'Yes, thank you,' he turned to the mother. 'That's a fine baby you've got there, and a good pair of lungs too!'

They all laughed, three people briefly united by the miracle of birth, and then Martin went out again. It couldn't possibly have been more ordinary. In future, Laura told herself firmly, she would keep it that way.

CHAPTER FIVE

MARTIN's words about Laura liking to have her life 'all nice and tidy' rankled for several days. Surely there was nothing wrong in wanting things to be orderly? It didn't have to mean you had no sense of adventure.

As she brooded over the accusation, she thought of her aunt, the district nurse. Miss Marsden had lived in Lavender Cottage and worked in the neighbourhood for thirty years. She had appeared to have been well content, and certainly she'd been well-loved, but nobody could have called her life exciting.

Suddenly Laura was frightened. She didn't want to be like that. She wanted to fall in love with some man who meant all the world to her, marry him and bear his children. And yet some people would consider that a dull programme. Martin, for instance.

Her thoughts inevitably switched to Lucy Goring. She must have married at seventeen and quickly borne two children, and now she was getting divorced and had another child whose father was very likely not the man she had married. Although she seemed happy enough now, it didn't appear that she had known much happiness in the past.

More confused than ever, Laura abandoned her soul-searching and came to a sudden decision. She might not be able to do much to make her life more exciting, but at least she could throw a party. Ever since she had moved in, people had been dropping hints about a house-warming and now that she had got the house straight, if still some-what bare, there was no reason to delay any longer.

'You'll help me, won't you?' she said to Jenny when she had announced her plans. 'And I expect Anita will too, provided we can fix an evening when we're all off duty.'

They were talking in the kitchen as they put out cups and saucers for the patients' tea, the orderly being off sick. Neither of them minded the menial task since it gave them an opportunity for conver-sation while the rooms were full of visitors.

'Are you going to invite particular people to your party or just issue a general invitation?' Jenny asked, turning up the urn to 'high'.

'I think invitations are best, but I want to be elastic about them, of course. I'm going to put Gavin at the top of the list, followed by Jonathan and Nick, but I don't suppose all three of them will be able to come. Obviously they can't be bleeped as far away as Mayes. Who shall I put next?'

'Your neighbour across the green,' Jenny said promptly.

'Martin Kent? You're joking! Consultants don't come to nurses' parties.'

'Most of them don't, but Martin is still young. I think you ought to ask him, since you live so near.'

Laura was not at all sure she wanted to but perhaps it would be bad manners to leave him out. He probably wouldn't come anyway. 'I shall have to invite Lucy as well,' she pointed out.

'Why?'

'It's obvious, surely! They're living—er—in the same house, so I can't not ask her.' About to add that she had received hospitality at Hill House, she remembered she had told no one about that surprise invitation.

'I've got a kind of gut feeling,' Jenny said hesitantly, 'that you don't much want either of them at your party. Am I right?'

'Of course you're not! I couldn't care less. Locally, as far as I'm concerned, they're just part of the village scene.'

And just to convince herself that what she had said really was true, she looked for an early opportunity of mentioning the party to Martin.

It occurred one lunchtime when she was waiting for the lift to take her down to the ground floor. When it arrived noiselessly and the doors slid back, she found Martin alone inside. He was in theatre gear, except for a mask, the green cap pushed untidily back and the V-neck of the smock showing dark curling hair on his chest. Surprised to see him—though there was no reason why she should be since the lift had just come down from theatres—Laura reacted to the impact of his presence in a way that caused her considerable annoyance.

He said 'Hi!' in a casual tone, his mind obviously on weightier matters and, to cover her quite ridiculous confusion, she burst into speech.

'I'm throwing a party next Wednesday at Lavender Cottage—a sort of house-warming. I'd be very pleased if you and Lucy could come.'

'A house-warming?' His eyes suddenly came alive and twinkled at her. 'How very enterprising of you, Laura.'

The lift stopped and they both got out, squeezing past a mobile bed with a patient in it, pushed by two porters. Not liking the tone of his comment, Laura felt herself flushing.

'Are you free on Wednesday?' she demanded.

'I think so but I don't know about Lucy. I'll have to ask her. Do you want me to let you know definitely or can we just turn up?'

'Just turn up, of course.' Laura was alarmed. 'Please don't let her think it's a formal party of the kind she's probably used to. Hospital parties aren't a bit like that.'

'I'm not so ancient that I can't remember,' he pointed out drily, adding over his shoulder and with a return to his casual manner, 'Thanks for the invitation.'

Glad to have that behind her, Laura continued on her way to the canteen. That evening she began her preparations, knowing that she wouldn't have much time off until her free day next week, which was Wednesday. By the weekend everything in the cottage was clean and unnaturally tidy and she was well aware that she would find it a strain keeping it like that. It was a waste of time really, she reflected, since five minutes after the party started there would be chaos everywhere.

On Sunday she was on duty all day, and they almost had mothers queueing up for the delivery-room. The next few days were similarly busy, and seemed to fly by.

On the day of the party Luara was up early, feeling that she ought to be busy but not quite sure what she should be doing. The house was already clean, but she watered her indoor plants and urged them to look their best and then went out shopping. There was a miniature supermarket in Mayes so she did not have to drive into the town. She was only intending to offer bread and cheese, and various extras like watercress, celery and grapes, relying on her guests to provide the drink.

She was returning to the cottage, laden with two large carrier-bags and wishing she had taken the car, when Martin's BMW stopped beside her.

'You look a bit loaded,' he commented, getting out and coming round to join her on the path. 'Get in the car and I'll drive you home.'

'I'm fine, thanks,' Laura said swiftly. 'I've got everything nicely balanced.'

He muttered something she didn't catch and then continued more audibly, 'That doesn't mean the weight's not too much for you. It's quite a long time since I had anything to do with orthopaedics, but I know it's a strain on the back of the neck to carry heavy loads, so hand those bags over at once and don't argue.'

If he had not been so domineering, Laura would have obeyed without further argument. As it was, her chin lifted slightly. 'I'm perfectly all right, thank you. I've only got to walk round the green and——'

But Martin was blocking her way. For a long moment he looked down on her, his steely gaze holding hers, and then he removed the two heavy bags from her grasp. 'Doctor's orders!' he said curtly.

Laura's cheeks were already flushed with exertion and now they burned brighter still, but to resist him would have been ridiculous and so she yielded without attempting a struggle. In silence she watched him put her shopping in the boot, and then got in beside him.

A few seconds later she got out again and waited to regain possession, only to find he was determined to carry the bags into the kitchen for her.

'Nice little place,' he said, looking round at gleaming white tiles, old-fashioned wooden draining-board and well-scrubbed table. 'Not too clinical. I like that geranium you've got on the window-sill. It reminds me of my mother's kitchen.'

'My aunt was very good with pot plants,' Laura told him, and found herself wondering whether Lucy was.

'Mind if I look round the ground floor?'

'There's only one other room and a small lobby, and you'll see them both this evening—if you're coming.'

'We hope to, provided nothing crops up to prevent us.' He was already off on his tour of inspection, ignoring her hint that he should wait until later. 'I've sometimes thought I'd like one of these little places,' he went on, standing in the middle of the sitting-room and dwarfing it. 'Somehow a cottage is much more interesting than a flat.'

Laura stood still in the doorway and stared at him. 'But you don't live in a flat,' she said stupidly.

'Who says I don't?'

'Nobody.' She floundered hopelessly. 'I mean— well, you live at Hill House. That's not a flat.'

'Granted.' He seemed amused at her confusion. 'But it so happens that at some time in its life a granny flat was added at the back and, since Lucy's mother hasn't reached that stage and didn't need it, it seemed a good idea for me to take it over when I was appointed to the local hospital. It's just as suitable for a bachelor as for a granny.'

'I see,' Laura said breathlessly and wondered how much she actually saw.

It was impossible not to be glad that Martin didn't, technically, share Lucy's house, but it didn't necessarily mean they weren't lovers, only that they were being a little more discreet than the hospital gave them credit for.

It was devastating to find her momentary spurt of happiness dissolving again within a few seconds, and she couldn't help being angry with herself *because* she had been so glad. There was no reason for it. Absolutely none. The relationship between Martin and Lucy was nothing to do with her. Nothing at all.

'Time I was going.' Martin made a move towards the door. 'Hang on a minute—I've got a contribution towards the party in the car.'

He hurried down the path and reappeared a moment later with a bottle of red wine which he thrust at Laura. 'Don't go and stick it in the fridge,' he warned. 'Red wine should be drunk at room temperature.'

'I know that!' She was annoyed at the unnecessary advice. 'I'll treat your bottle with the respect which it deserves, and——' her tone was suddenly unnaturally sweet '—thank you *very* much for bringing it.'

Martin regarded her thoughtfully. 'You seem very edgy this afternoon. Are you nervous about tonight? I'm sure there's no need to be.' A wicked twinkle gleamed in his eyes. 'I'd prescribe some more of that therapy we had the other Sunday, but neither of us has the time just now. Pity.'

And with a broad smile he departed.

* * *

The party went with a swing right from the beginning. Laura allotted no part of its success to herself, since hospital parties were nearly always successful. Everyone knew everyone else and nobody felt out of it when people talked shop, which they did most of the time.

Occasionally she worried a little about the noise and hoped her neighbours were charitable. Rather more frequently, she wondered why Martin hadn't turned up and hoped he hadn't been held up by some crisis at the hospital.

'You girls want any help?' Jonathan appeared in the kitchen where Jenny and Laura were washing glasses.

'No, thanks,' Laura said hastily, removing the lipstick from the rim of a glass with great care. 'You're too big to be allowed in here, so scram!'

He looked down at his hands and flexed the fingers. 'If I can handle newborn babies, I can surely be trusted with a few glasses.'

'Babies are much stronger than glass, and in any case we've nearly finished.'

He withdrew obediently, but when they emerged a little later they found him propping up the wall nearby.

'They're trying to organise some dancing,' he told them. 'There isn't room but who cares about that?'

Someone had turned the volume up and music now dominated the general uproar. Laura found herself gathered into a powerful embrace and held in a bear-like hug. Her face was pressed into Jonathan's chest and she felt she could hardly breathe.

'Jonathan—please!' she begged faintly.

He peered down at her. 'What a little thing you are! I've never noticed before.'

'I'm not really. It's because you're so big.'

Steered into the centre of the room, with slowly gyrating couples all round, Laura had a panicky feeling of being trapped. It was so hot, and not only her partner but everybody else seemed to be towering over her, even though she wasn't all that small. She made a convulsive movement towards escape but it was useless. Jonathan didn't relax his grip in the slightest. He probably wouldn't even have noticed if she'd fainted in his arms.

Not a girl who was given to fainting, Laura steeled herself to endure her ordeal. Just as she was really getting desperate, relief came.

'My turn, I think,' said a voice above her head, and suddenly there was space and air between her face and Jonathan's chest as his arms dropped. They were replaced by a different pair which held her much more comfortably.

'For a girl who, I suspect, prides herself on standing firmly on her own two feet,' Martin said conversationally, 'you seem to need an awful lot of rescuing. Twice in one day is a bit excessive, don't you think?'

'You!' she gasped. 'I didn't know you were here.'

'You're not out of date by more than a minute or two. Anyway, you haven't been in a position to take much note of new arrivals just lately.'

'You can say that again!' She laughed and then demanded, 'What did you mean about rescuing me twice?'

'Have you forgotten the shopping?'

'I told you I didn't need any help——'

'So you did, and *I* told *you* that I knew better. You're not going to start the argument all over again, are you?' He looked down suddenly and gave her a penetrating stare.

'Of course not.' Lowering her lashes hastily, she returned her gaze to a scrutiny of the fawn silk shirt which had replaced Jonathan's crumpled stripes. Being held in his arms like this was doing strange things to her heartbeats and against her will her mind went winging off to the 'therapy' he had referred to earlier. She had been almost frightened then by the intensity of her erotic feelings, and yet she had known all the time that it meant nothing. Martin had made it quite clear that it was merely an enjoyable interlude and she had known he was right.

So why did she feel right now as though they were alone on a desert island, just the two of them, instead of being surrounded by bodies? And, presumably, with his girlfriend around somewhere. She must be mad!

'Do you really want to continue with this pretence at dancing? There simply isn't room for it,' he said abruptly.

'I agree.' Steered to the fringe of the crowd, Laura slipped out of his arms with an odd mixture of relief and regret. 'Come and have a drink and something to eat.'

They found Lucy in the kitchen talking to Jenny and eating crisps. It was the first time Laura had seen her since her surprise invitation to supper and she would hardly have recognised her. The lank mousy hair had been brightened and expertly cut, her blue-grey eyes had been skilfully glamourised and given an added sparkle, and her normally pale skin was delicately tinted.

'You're looking absolutely blooming!' she exclaimed. 'How's the baby?'

'Lorraine is doing fine. I can honestly say she's never given me a moment's anxiety. I'm sure babies have a sixth sense about being wanted, don't you?'

In Laura's limited experience babies didn't have a sixth sense about anything except the need for food, but she was careful to go along with the suggestion. On the surface anyway.

Inside, her mind was in turmoil. If Lucy said the baby was wanted, surely her husband *couldn't* have been the father since Lorraine must have been conceived when they were already thinking about divorce. That, as far as she knew, left only Martin.

She stole a glance at him but he had moved away to speak to a staff nurse from the obstetrics ward. They were drinking some of his red wine and laughing together. And, as Laura gazed at his clear-cut profile and crisp, slightly wavy hair, his lean narrow-hipped body with its suggestion of powerful muscles, she knew—without the slightest shadow of doubt—that she couldn't bear to think of him as the father of Lucy's child.

Standing there, alone in the midst of her guests, she had an insane and very nearly irresistible desire to burst into tears.

With superhuman self-control, Laura returned her attention to Lucy, only to find she was talking about Martin.

'He's been an absolute tower of strength to me since my husband left. I really don't know what I would have done without him. He deals with my tax difficulties, and insurance and car problems—all that sort of thing. Only a few high-powered businesswomen are capable of coping with all that boring side of life, and I'm certainly not one of those.'

No one would have suspected that she was, Laura reflected, not unkindly. Aloud she said, 'You don't mind being bossed around?'

Lucy looked surprised. 'Oh, no, I rather like it. It gives a girl a marvellous sense of security, don't you think so?'

'I—I don't know. I haven't had much experience of it.' And what she had had, she hadn't liked, she added silently to herself. Or was that just because she was fighting against something—and someone—which threatened to dominate her life?

'You haven't got a boyfriend?' Lucy was asking.

Laura shook her head emphatically. 'I've steered clear of men for the last couple of years and concentrated on nursing. Before that I had a few light-hearted affairs.'

'How old are you?'

'I was twenty-three a few weeks ago. On the day Lorraine was born.'

'I'd forgotten it was your birthday.' Lucy cut a slice of cheese and balanced it on a piece of crusty French bread. 'Just think—I'm only a year older and I've got three children. But I wouldn't recommend it. I think you're very wise to wait until you're more mature. You're not so likely to make a mistake.'

But Laura was afraid that she was making the biggest mistake in her whole life.

CHAPTER SIX

IN THE morning Laura surveyed the state of her house and shuddered. Jenny had helped with most of the washing-up but she had been getting a lift in Jonathan's car and could not keep him waiting too long. Anita had not turned up at all, but neither of her friends was surprised that she had obviously not been able to get away.

After a whole day off Laura was on early duty so she had to leave everything as it was until the evening, which was depressing. Added to that, it was raining, and she managed to convince herself that these two things were responsible for her low spirits.

Another was to be added when she set out for the hospital. Her car was reluctant to start.

She got it going eventually and set out for the hospital determined to leave it at the garage in Wickenfield to have some new plugs fitted. All the time she had been trying to get the engine to fire she had been desperately afraid that Martin would come along and perform another of his rescuing acts. She just couldn't have borne it!

The garage promised to have the car ready by lunchtime and Laura walked quickly along the main road to the pedestrain crossing opposite the

Monk's Head and went over in a crowd of other people. Suddenly, behind her, she heard the screech of brakes.

As she swung round, she saw a girl lying still in the road and a familiar car halted at an angle just beyond. Martin's car.

She thought she knew the girl too. It was a red-headed young student nurse named Sally Milne from the surgical ward where Anita worked. The bright hair was rapidly turning a different shade of red as blood welled from a gash on her head.

All around people were staring, momentarily shocked into immobility. With a muttered, 'Excuse me, please,' Laura pushed her way to the front and ran across to the prone figure.

Martin was there already, on his knees beside the girl. He was feeling her head gently, trying to discover whether there was anything worse than a bad cut. As Laura joined him he glanced at her briefly. 'Her skull seems all right, as far as I can tell without an X-ray.' His hands moved on to explore the limbs, making sure that there were no fractures.

At his side Laura found a clean handkerchief and carefully wiped away the blood which was streaming down the girl's ashen face. She might come round in a minute and she'd be terrified to find herself blinded by the red flow.

'I can't find anything else wrong.' Martin was clearly relieved. 'She's very lucky, streaking across like that after the lights had changed. It was fortunate I'd only just started off and wasn't driving fast.' He looked at Laura. 'I suppose you've asked somebody to send for an ambulance?'

'Well, n-no—I just ran back to see if I could help.'

'And you a nurse!' he exclaimed scathingly.

'That's why I wanted to help,' Laura snapped back at him.

At that moment a new voice above their heads joined in the conversation. 'The ambulance has been summoned, sir, and it's not likely to be long seeing as it's only got to come a few hundred yards.' The policeman produced a notebook. 'I'd like a statement from you both, please.'

The ambulance arrived just then with a shriek from its siren and, while the victim was being loaded in, Laura stole a peep at her watch. If she didn't want to be late, she would have to get away at once and run all the way to the maternity block too. There was really no reason why she should stay—she hadn't been a witness.

But the policeman was assuming that she was involved. There was no way he would let her go until she had made some sort of statement. He had taken Martin's first, since he was the driver of the car concerned, and was writing it down slowly and carefully. In a moment it would be her turn.

'Now, miss—name and address, please.' He wrote them in his notebook with maddening slowness. 'I see you're both from Mayes. Were you together in the car, then?'

'I was on foot,' Laura said quickly.

'But you did see what happened?'

To Laura the slight pause seemed to go on for ever. She knew the policeman had noticed it because he glanced up with his pen poised and gave her a questioning look. 'Oh, yes,' she heard herself saying calmly. 'I had only just crossed myself and I saw it all.'

'Then I'd like your version, if you please.'

Fortunately her ears had retained the gist of what Martin had told him and she was able to corroborate it without difficulty. 'It was just as Mr Kent said. The pedestrian light had turned to red and all the held-up traffic was starting off, and then the girl rushed across right in front of everything. It was a crazy thing to do.'

The officer studied her gravely. 'You definitely saw this? If you'd just crossed yourself, I would have expected you to have had your back turned.'

Laura's mind worked like lightning and she could only hope that it didn't show in her face.

'I was one of the last to get over,' she explained carefully. 'The amber light was flashing at the time. Then when I reached the kerb I turned left towards the hospital and I saw the red light out of the corner of my eye, and—and the girl too. The next thing I heard was the shriek of brakes.'

'Out of the corner of your eye,' the man wrote down solemnly. 'Thank you, miss. That'll be all for the present.'

'I hope you've finished with me too,' Martin said impatiently.

'Oh, yes, sir—for the time being anyway. Thank you for your co-operation.'

Laura turned and fled, running like the wind towards the gates, through them and up the long sloping driveway. She had not gone far, but was already panting, when she heard a car stopping beside her.

'You'd better get in,' Martin said. 'It might save you a few seconds.'

'But I'm nearly there——'

'*Get in*!' he roared furiously and she did so hastily. As she collapsed beside him, he added disapprovingly, 'You're shockingly out of condition.'

'I don't often run anywhere so of course I'm out of practice,' Laura panted.

'I prescribe a course of jogging before breakfast.'

She forced a smile. 'Perhaps I might think about it when I'm not on early duty.'

Martin made no further comment, but when they were walking together towards the entrance of the maternity block he said suddenly, 'I suppose you know you're a damned little fool?'

She turned an indignant face towards him. 'What on earth do you mean?'

'Only that if the police make a case of that accident and it comes to court, you'll either have to retract your evidence or commit perjury. You didn't see anything at all, did you?'

'I—I heard the brakes——'

'Don't be daft. It's not the same thing at all.'

Laura pulled herself together. 'How do you know I wasn't really a witness?'

'I was watching you cross while I waited and noticed you were deep in thought. When you reached the kerb you were swallowed up by the crowd. Then the amber light stopped flashing and I began to move off. The rest you know.' And as she remained silent, he added very quietly, 'Why did you do it, Laura? It's never a good idea to lie to the police.'

But she had no intention of telling him the reason behind her instinctive action, so she merely shrugged and hurried ahead of him into the building.

Sister was at the nurses' station when she went into the ward. She looked up and the dark penetrating eyes seemed to bore right into Laura's secret thoughts.

'And what have you to say for yourself, Nurse Marsden? I suppose you're aware it's ten minutes past eight and you should have been here at seven-thirty?'

'Yes, of course, Sister, but——'

'Last time you were late, I remember, you had most unnecessarily got yourself involved with an expectant mother. It will be interesting to hear your excuse this time.'

'This time it was a street accident,' Laura told her with a shade of defiance in her tone. 'I was a

Mills & Boon

Discover FREE BOOKS AND FREE GIFTS
From Mills & Boon

As a special introduction to Mills & Boon Romances we will send you:

FOUR FREE Mills & Boon Romances plus a FREE TEDDY and MYSTERY GIFT when you return this card.

But first - just for fun - see if you can find and circle four hidden words in the puzzle.

R	D	A	V	R	Y	B	X	N	M
B	O	O	K	N	C	A	S	P	Y
Z	G	M	N	B	U	L	T	R	S
R	T	N	A	N	E	F	T	A	T
D	H	I	A	N	V	K	D	M	E
N	W	L	K	H	C	O	W	S	R
O	C	O	M	U	T	E	D	D	Y
I	L	V	F	L	P	B	I	T	E
F	E	E	J	S	G	I	F	T	P
S	P	N	S	E	T	I	N	R	E

The hidden words are:

MYSTERY
ROMANCE
TEDDY
GIFT

Now turn over to claim your
FREE BOOKS AND GIFTS

Free Books Certificate

Yes! Please send me four specially selected Mills & Boon Romances, together with my FREE Teddy and Mystery Gift. I would also like you to reserve a special Reader Service Subscription for me. Which means that I can go on to enjoy six brand new Romances sent to me each month for just £8.70, postage and packing FREE. If I decide not to subscribe I shall write to you within 10 days. Any FREE books and gifts will remain mine to keep. I understand that I am under no obligation whatsoever - I can cancel or suspend my subscription at any time simply by writing to you. I am over 18 years of age.

4A1R

FREE TEDDY

MYSTERY GIFT

mps MAILING PREFERENCE SERVICE

Mrs/Miss/Mr _____

Address _____

_____

_____ Postcode _____

Signature _____

witness and I had to make a statement to the police.'

'Didn't you tell the officer you were a nurse on your way to work?'

'It wouldn't have made any difference.'

'That's a matter of opinion. The police, if treated rightly, are usually reasonable beings. You could have given your statement some other time.'

But if she had had time to think she might not have given it at all. Shying away from that, Laura said merely, 'I'm very sorry, Sister.'

'So am I, and I hope it won't happen again. You may go.'

Laura escaped with relief. On her way to the babies' room she met one of the midwives.

'Whatever happened to you? Did you have a hangover after your party?'

'Of course not!' Laura smiled and gave a brief account of her adventure.

'I bet Sister tore you off a strip. Some nurses won't stand for that sort of treatment nowadays, and a younger sister wouldn't dare to try it on. Leggett is a relic of the dark ages of nursing and thank goodness we shan't have to put up with her much longer. I happen to know she's fifty-nine.'

'She looked more than that this morning.'

'Poor old thing,' the midwife said charitably. 'She's obviously past it and, in my opinion, she should have taken early retirement.'

'I don't expect she'd want to do that. She loves the babies so much.'

'You're right there, and that reminds me—will you take charge in the nursery? We've got three mothers wanting to learn how to bath their infants this morning.'

Laura plunged into work and immersed herself totally. She was happy as she handled the babies and explained the finer points of their toilet. They had no problem mothers in the ward just now and the infants were all healthy.

Halfway through the morning her absorption was broken into by Martin's unexpected appearance in the kitchen, and immediately she was reminded of the unfortunate beginning to her day.

'Any coffee going?' he asked hopefully. 'I've got to go across to theatres and I could do with a cup first.'

'Since when have they stopped serving coffee over there?'

'As far as I know it's still on tap, but I fancy a cup here. Any objection?'

'Oh, no,' Laura told him lightly. 'It's a pleasure.'

'I'm glad to hear it. I was beginning to have serious doubts.'

'Who are you operating on?' she enquired as she poured hot water on to instant coffee.

'A woman who's just been rushed in. An ectopic. Apart from the pain and general unpleasantness, I gather she doesn't mind all that much about the foetus developing in the wrong place. She's got five children already and doesn't want any more.' Leaning against the table, he began to sip his coffee.

Laura wondered whether she dared get some for herself, in spite of having already had her break, but decided it wouldn't be wise with Sister in her present mood.

'Have you any news of Sally Milne?' she asked, to break the silence.

'Who? Oh, you mean the girl who tried to commit suicide at the traffic lights——?'

'You're not serious?'

'Good heavens, no! Just a figure of speech. I rang up A and E and they said she'd been X-rayed and was suffering from nothing more than concussion and shock, apart from the gash on her head, of course. I reckon she caught the wing of my car and was flung clear.'

'That was lucky for her.'

'Considering what an idiot she was being, I suppose it was.' He drank thirstily and then changed the subject. 'It was a good party, Laura. Lucy enjoyed it immensely in spite of knowing hardly anybody—in fact, she's talking about giving one herself.'

'Really?' Laura exclaimed. 'Do you mean another hospital party?'

'Oh, yes, but I don't think it would be a good idea. If you remove a medical crowd too far from the hospital scene, it's likely to fall apart. Most people feel a bit awkward about talking shop when the hostess can't join in and they'd have difficulty in thinking of anything else to talk about. I shall do my best to dissuade her.'

'I expect you'll be successful.' There was a shade of sarcasm in Laura's voice.

'Probably.' His tone seemed to her to be disgustingly complacent. 'She usually takes my advice.'

'It must be nice to have someone who does that, without arguing about it.'

Martin raised his dark eyebrows and studied her across the top of his cup. 'It certainly makes a nice change,' he said smoothly.

Laura flushed and suddenly remembered she was in the kitchen for the purpose of mixing a bottle for a hungry baby whose mother's milk supply was inadequate. By the time she had collected what she needed, Martin had gone.

The pressure of work eased and she wasn't able to put him so completely out of her mind. At lunchtime she joined Jenny and Anita in the canteen and immediately told them about the accident.

'Sally Milne's always doing something crazy,' Anita commented. 'She comes from the back of beyond—Orkney or Shetland—where traffic is practically non-existent. She just doesn't seem able to cope with a busy town.'

'Perhaps this will teach her that a red light means what it says,' Jenny suggested.

'Perhaps.' Anita looked dubious. 'I'd like to think she'll be more careful in future because she's not a bad kid. I wonder how soon she'll be able to have visitors?'

'Martin said she'd got concussion so if you're thinking of visiting her you'd better wait a couple of days at least.' Laura tackled her chicken curry hungrily and then added, 'Would you mind if I came with you? I feel a sort of proprietory interest.'

'Because of witnessing the accident?'

'You could put it like that.'

Laura had given her friends the same version as the one she had dictated to the policeman, and had felt even more uncomfortable about deceiving them than she had about deceiving the police.

Three days later, discovering that both had a free afternoon, Laura and Anita went to see Sally.

The Sick Bay was a large ward on the top floor of one of the wings. It consisted of single rooms and larger ones with three or four beds in them, and had a pleasant outlook towards the trees of the local park.

'Sally Milne?' the staff nurse in charge said doubtfully. 'The concussion was severe but I suppose you can go in for a few minutes, since her folks are too far away to visit her. Are you particular friends of hers?'

'I'm on the same ward,' Anita explained, and Laura added her own reason for being there.

'Don't say anything about the accident,' the staff nurse warned them. 'Not unless you have to, that is—you may find Sally wants to talk about it.' She looked straight at Laura. 'And, whatever you do, don't disagree with her. As far as we're concerned, her idea of what happened is correct.'

Sally was in one of the small rooms and still in bed. She looked pale and ill, with a severe bruise on her forehead and part of her bright hair shaved off, revealing a line of stitches. On the locker a large vase of irises and freesias filled the air with sweetness. She looked vaguely at her visitors and then recognised Anita.

'Hi, there!' the black girl said with a smile. 'How are you doing, then?'

'I'm feeling absolutely lousy. My head still aches and I can't read or do anything except listen to the radio.'

'I'm not surprised after a bash like that, but you'll be a lot better in a few days.'

'Of course you will,' Laura said warmly as they sat down uninvited. It hadn't been a good idea to visit the accident victim. She could see that now.

'You're my first visitors,' Sally told them dolefully, 'but I spoke to my mother on the phone last night. I wish she wasn't so far away——' Tears welled up in her eyes. 'I'd love to see her right now.'

Anita switched the conversation to the flowers. 'Somebody seems to think a lot of you.' She stood up and bent to smell the freesias. 'These are lovely.'

To the surprise of both visitors, Sally frowned,

winced and then leaned her head languidly against the pillows.

'Mr Kent sent them. I can't think why he bothered. Nobody in their right mind would believe that a bunch of expensive flowers could make up for knocking someone down on a pedestrian crossing.'

There was a short uncomfortable pause, and then Laura said gently, 'I'm sure he didn't mean it that way. I expect they were just a—a gesture. Because he was sorry you'd been hurt.'

'You mean because he'd hurt me, don't you?' Sally stared at them, her voice stronger and definitely challenging.

Laura hesitated, the nurse's injunction clear in her mind. The girl was still confused, that was very plain. Almost certainly as the effects of the concussion wore off she would remember exactly what had happened and how foolishly she had acted. 'Put it that way if you like,' she said with a smile. 'Whatever his reason for sending them, the flowers are beautiful.' The violence of Sally's reply alarmed her.

'Do you know what I'd like to do? I'd like to open the window and throw them out—every single one of them! And I'd like Mr Kent to see me doing it.' The pale cheeks were suffused with colour.

There was another awkward pause and then Anita got up decisively. 'Time we were going. We were warned not to tire you and I think we've stayed long enough.'

'You'll come again?' the patient begged with sudden pathos.

'If that's what you want, but I expect you'll get lots of visitors as soon as you're well enough. Goodbye for now.'

They did not speak until they had left the ward and then Laura burst out explosively, 'I knew concussion frequently caused amnesia but I didn't think it could result in fantasy!'

'You think it would have been more normal if Sally had simply been unable to remember anything at all about the accident?'

'Yes, I do. I can't think where this fixation on Martin being entirely to blame came from. It really is most unfair.'

Anita glanced at her curiously. 'I don't expect he'll let it worry him too much, so there's no need for you to get so steamed up about it. As for the fixation, it's my belief that when she came round somebody told her she'd been knocked down on a pedestrian crossing—which was true enough. She simply assumed it was the motorist's fault.'

'So it's really amnesia after all?'

'Certainly could be,' Anita said indifferently. 'It doesn't matter all that much, does it? The police presumably know the truth so there's not likely to be a court case.'

But *did* the police know the facts? Laura wondered as she left the hospital to do some shopping.

Had they really accepted her testimony or were they fully aware that it was false?

'How did you find Sally?' Jenny asked when they met after Laura's return to duty.

'She's still suffering from concussion. In fact, I'm surprised we were allowed in.'

'You sound a bit cheesed off. Is anything wrong?'

'Of course not! What could be wrong?'

'Perhaps you're suffering from reaction after the success of your party. Shall we go across to the Monk tonight and have a mildly convivial evening? We haven't been there together since you moved out to Mayes. Perhaps Anita will come too.'

But, when the time came for leaving, Jenny went alone to look for Anita as Laura was busy with a new admission. 'Mrs Adams is terribly nervous,' she explained, standing outside the labour-room with her hand on the door-handle. 'I must stay with her until she settles down, but I don't expect I shall be long.'

'See you at the Monk, then,' Jenny said without argument.

It was nearly an hour before Laura was ready to leave and she felt strangely disinclined for what Jenny had called a 'mildly convivial evening'. For one thing, it was very warm—almost summer-like—and not yet fully dark, although a single star shone brightly in the east.

Even in the middle of the town, and with the

great block of the hospital all around, there was a feeling of pulsating life. Out in the country everything would be growing, thrusting out leaves and flowers and strong new roots, and suddenly Laura longed to be part of it. She had only to get in her car and drive home, instead of going to the Monk's Head, she reminded herself, and she would be in the country.

But somehow that wasn't what she wanted. A wilder longing had taken possession of her—to walk by the sea and listen to the waves, to wander over the heath and feel the wind in her hair. But it wouldn't be much fun alone, even if she was mad enough to do it.

In fact, if she wasn't with the right person, it would be no fun at all.

She was standing on the edge of the car park, dithering, when a voice spoke quietly from behind her.

'They must be remarkably weighty thoughts to freeze you into immobility like that. Have you got some terrible problem to solve?'

'Yes, I have!' Laura spun round and faced Martin, bursting into slightly hysterical laughter to hide the effect on her of his abrupt appearance. 'I'm trying to make up my mind whether to go home or meet some friends in the Monk. It's a very difficult decision indeed.'

'I can appreciate that,' he said solemnly, 'since I'm at this moment grappling with a similar

decision. How would it be if we both did something quite different?'

'Such as what?' she asked breathlessly.

'Such as driving out to a different pub, one
considerably quieter than the Monk, and having a
drink there. Does the idea appeal to you?'

It appealed so much that Laura, in an attempt to
hide it from him, found herself pretending to
hesitate. 'Jenny and Anita will wonder what's
happened to me.'

'Let them.' Martin slipped his arm into hers and
drew her towards the consultants' special car park.
'Where would you like to go?'

With his usual assurance, he seemed to have
taken her agreement for granted, but Laura felt
in no mood to protest. 'I was just longing for
the real country, somewhere a bit less suburban
than Mayes, where there are lovely country
smells——'

'Country smells aren't always attractive.' There
was a ripple of laughter in his voice. 'But we'll try
to dodge fertiliser and pigs tonight. What would
you really like? Hawthorn and wild roses? I'm
afraid it's a bit too early for those but I'll do my
best to find something pleasing.'

Laura got into the car and leaned back with a
sigh. 'I'll leave it to you,' she murmured dreamily.

At her side she could sense his astonishment.
'No arguments?' he asked incredulously. 'I don't
believe it! To what do we owe this surprising
transformation?'

But although Laura knew the answer, she locked it away in her heart and refused to acknowledge it even to herself.

CHAPTER SEVEN

THE Red Lion was in the centre of a small village near the river, a pretty little thatched place with tubs of budding geraniums along the front. The car park was nearly empty, and as she got out of the car an atmosphere of peace and quiet seemed to enfold Laura. She walked into the bar beside Martin in a haze of inexplicable contentment and the next hour seemed equally unreal.

She was well aware that she was surrounded by dark panelled walls and dangling horse brasses, and that a cheerful—but quite unnecessary—log fire burned on the hearth. It was all very pleasant but not in the least important. What really mattered was the extraordinary fact that she was there with Martin.

How could she possibly have imagined that she didn't like him? He was a different person from the autocratic young consultant she had hitherto known and fought with—quietly attentive and interesting to talk to. He told her about his home in London and listened with genuine interest to her description of the village near Canterbury where her parents lived.

'Did you never want to be a teacher too?' he asked.

'Oh, no—it was always going to be nursing for me and I've never regretted the choice for a single moment, not even in my first year. I like looking after people and making them more comfortable when they're in pain and frightened.' Colour flooded her face as she realised what a sentimental picture she was drawing. He would look upon such an attitude as unspeakably corny. 'I'm sorry.' She lowered her eyes in embarrassment. 'Nurses are supposed to be cool, calm and detached.'

'They should be cool and calm in their behaviour and still let the patient know there's an inner warmth. As for being detached, that's a personal thing for their own protection. They'd never stay the course if they didn't practise a certain amount of detachment. The same applies to doctors.'

'I should think it's easier for them.'

'Up to a point,' he admitted. 'Are you going to continue with midwifery when you've completed Part I?'

Laura shook her head. 'I'm enjoying the course but I really prefer more varied nursing. I think I'd like to be a staff nurse on a medical ward—that's *real* nursing!'

They sat in silence for a moment and then Martin roused himself. 'Like another drink?'

When she refused, he stood up at once. 'We'd better start back or your friends will be organising a search party.'

Not turning up at the Monk was going to take a bit of explaining, Laura reflected as they left the pub. Shelving the problem for the moment, she got into the car, but as they drove towards Wickenfield she could feel her mood changing as palpably as though it were a physical thing. The magic was dissolving like mist in the sunshine and by the time the orange glow in the sky ahead of them had turned into chains of separate lights she was back to normal. It seemed quite impossible that there could ever have been those strange moments of sympathy and understanding between herself and Martin as they had sat quietly talking in the Red Lion.

'Thank you very much,' she said politely when he stopped to let her out. 'I really enjoyed that.'

'We both needed a change of scene.'

'Yes.' She put out her hand to undo the door and fumbled a little. Martin leaned across to undo it for her, or so she thought, and his nearness immediately set her heart pounding so that she had difficulty in controlling her breathing. And then, instead of opening the door, he slid his hand upwards and turned her head to face him. She could feel his other hand at the back of her neck and between the two of them there was no escaping the urgency of his mouth.

Not that Laura wanted to escape. She had not realised how vulnerable she was after that short spell of happiness in the quiet country pub. Her whole body had responded instantly to his kiss and she felt a desperate longing for fulfilment—a longing so crazy that, at the same time, she experienced a burning sense of shame.

She would never know fulfilment with Martin. Never. He belonged to Lucy and somehow she must steel herself not to forget it even for one moment.

Instead of being a willing partner she began to struggle.

Martin raised his head abruptly. 'I'm sorry—I forgot.' His voice was harsh and bitter. 'You don't like being mauled. My apologies, Laura. If I'd remembered in time I wouldn't have attempted to say goodnight to you in what most people regard as a perfectly normal manner.'

Suddenly she was free and the door swung open. Without a word she scrambled out of the car and fled towards her own. As she struggled to find the key, the hated word 'mauled' pounded through her head. Why on earth had she ever used it? Any man would regard it as an insult, and the last thing she had ever wanted was to insult Martin.

It seemed a miracle that she arrived back safely at Lavender Cottage that evening. It was as though the old Rover had been switched over to automatic pilot and it faithfully delivered her at her own gate. Mentally bruised and battered but with one thing clear in her mind, she went straight upstairs to bed.

There had now been two incidents in Martin's car which, though enjoyable at the time, had been painful and deeply regretted afterwards. She must at all costs avoid a third.

'Wherever did you get to last night?' Jenny demanded in the morning.

Laura had been so busy knocking sense into her rebellious mind and heart that she had omitted to provide herself with a reason for not turning up at the Monk. It was impossible to think of anything suitable on the spur of the moment and she had to fall back on telling the truth. Or some of it.

'I met Martin Kent on my way to the pub. He was going there too, but it was such a lovely evening that he suggested driving out into the country and having a drink somewhere quieter, so that's what we did.'

'But I thought you didn't like him?'

Laura shrugged. 'He's OK when he's not being bossy. I quite enjoyed it actually. It made a change.'

Jenny looked at her searchingly and then apparently accepted the explanation. 'In a way it was a pity he didn't come into the Monk. Somebody in our group had got hold of that story about his knocking Sally down on a pedestrian crossing. He could have stood up for himself and put matters straight.'

'I don't think he would have bothered,' Laura said thoughtfully, 'but you and Anita knew what actually happened. Why didn't you put people right?'

'We did try, but people weren't very interested. It didn't make nearly such a good story as the other one.'

'But it's not fair to say it was all his fault when he wasn't to blame at all,' Laura argued with unwise heat.

'That's what Gavin said. He knows Sally, being house surgeon on the same ward, and he thinks it's just the sort of thing she'd be likely to do—dashing across when the light was red.'

They were having coffee in the canteen during their break and Laura, anxious to switch the conversation from Martin, reminded her friend that it was time to return to the ward, and to gynaecological matters. Mrs Adams, the woman Laura had admitted just before she went off duty last night, was still in labour and her condition was causing concern. They were not surprised, when they got back, to find that Jonathan had sent for Martin.

Two more women in labour arrived, neither very advanced but they were allowed to remain since there were beds available for them though they were not expected to occupy them yet. The door of the delivery-room remained closed.

It was half an hour later that Laura heard how Mrs Adams's long ordeal had ended. She was in the nursery, gowned and masked, giving a bottle to a premature baby whose mother had gone home, when Martin came in. He was gowned, like her, but his mask was hanging below his chin and she could see that his expression was sombre.

'That little chap seems to be doing well,' he commented, standing at a little distance and watching her.

'Yes,' she agreed, showing no sign of what his sudden appearance had done to her. 'I expect he'll be going home to mum soon.'

There was a pause and then he said quietly, 'Some people aren't so lucky. The Adams baby was stillborn.'

'Oh, dear! I'm very sorry.'

'It does happen, you know, even in these days, though it's not very common, thank God.'

'Is she—very upset?'

'Of course!' He turned on her savagely. 'Wouldn't you be? I've had her moved to one of the single rooms, and I'd like to send her upstairs to the Obstetrics Department, right away from the sound of other people's live, healthy babies, but they say they haven't a bed at present.'

Laura was silent, understanding that he was angry and needed to take it out on somebody. She just wished it didn't have to be her. A memory from last night's conversation flashed into her mind. They had agreed that doctors usually found it easier to be detached than nurses. Martin wasn't showing much detachment at the moment.

He went on speaking. 'Apparently she's had several miscarriages, though she didn't tell us at first. She had great hopes of this baby because she'd managed to carry it to full term, so the disappointment is all the greater.'

Laura put down the empty bottle and expertly upended the baby into the approved 'burping' position. The tiny silken head nestled into her neck and she experienced a surge of emotion quite different from that which she had known last night.

Martin was watching her with a curious expression on his face. Then, with a shrug, he turned on his heel and left the nursery. Laura finished tending the baby and returned him to his cot. Back in the ward, she was surprised to find it was nearly lunchtime and flung herself into making sure that the patients were all ready when the heated trolley arrived.

She had just returned from her own lunch when she was accosted by Sister.

'One moment, Nurse Marsden.'

Half expecting to meet an accusing gaze— though she was unaware of any crime—Laura was distressed to see signs of strain on the drawn face confronting her. They all knew Sister Leggett wasn't very fit but she didn't usually show it as plainly as this.

'I appear to have eaten something which has disagreed with me, Nurse, and should appreciate the opportunity to lie down for an hour or so. As you know, there is no midwife on duty this after-noon and I don't usually leave the ward under those circumstances. However, I think you may have reached the stage when I can put you in charge for a short time. The two mothers we admitted this morning are proceeding normally and there will be a midwife available long before she is needed. You will, of course, undertake to send for me should an emergency occur. Is that understood?'

'Yes, of course, Sister. I'm sorry you don't feel well.'

'It will pass, no doubt, and the more quickly for a short rest.'

She must be feeling really ill to give in like that, Laura reflected as she went on her way. As for the responsibility which had so unexpectedly descended on herself, she was both pleased and slightly apprehensive. Jenny was off for the afternoon and there was no one whose advice she could ask, since the other nurses were all students, merely working in the ward and not doing their midwifery training. There was plenty of help at the other end of a telephone line but she didn't want to call on it unnecessarily.

At first all was peaceful. Mothers and babies were sleeping after lunch, and the two women in labour had both attended antenatal classes and were practising what they had been taught. The Obstetrics Department phoned down to say they had made room for Mrs Adams and she was dispatched to the floor above. After that the afternoon visitors began to pour in.

At about three o'clock the phone rang again and this time it was Accident and Emergency announcing that they had just admitted a maternity case who, like Lucy Goring, had gone into labour while out shopping. 'She's on her way now, Nurse,' said the voice at the other end. 'By the look of things there's no time to lose so I hope you're not too busy.'

Laura thought rapidly. If the new admission was as urgent as A and E seemed to think, perhaps she had better go straight to the delivery-room. After hesitating a moment, she decided not to call Sister immediately. She would assess the situation herself and then summon one of the housemen. Together they would make up their minds about the case.

Penny Johnson was nineteen and unmarried. She wore maternity trousers and a shapeless smock, and was probably quite pretty when she wasn't pregnant. At the moment her face glistened with sweat and there was a drawn look round her mouth. Her first utterance was a surprising one.

'You won't let Dave in, will you?' Hot hands clutched Laura's arm so fiercely that she had difficulty in freeing herself.

'Who's Dave?' she asked lightly.

'My boyfriend—I mean, he's not my boyfriend now, but he used to be and he's the father of the baby. I want to marry somebody else, see? And he's willing to adopt the kid but Dave doesn't want him to.'

'Don't worry, love—the baby will be *yours*. Er— do you want to see the other man if he turns up?'

'Course I do,' Penny said emphatically, 'only

not yet. I mean, it'd be embarrassing for him to be here while I'm in labour when the baby's not his. Do you know what I mean?' She collapsed with a groan as pain tore at her body.

'I understand perfectly so there's nothing for you to worry about except doing your part to help the baby along. And now I'm going to examine you and find out how far you've got.'

She felt the abdomen carefully and listened to the foetal heart. All seemed to be well, though the rate of progress was much faster than she would have liked and the dilation already considerable. 'I'm going to ask one of the doctors to take a look at you, Penny,' she said to the half-scared girl on the bed.

'There's something wrong?'

'Oh, no, it's just part of the routine. This infant of yours seems to be in rather a hurry.'

Nick arrived promptly and listened as Laura explained her problem—whether to call Sister at once or wait a little while—and then made his own assessment. 'I think you should summon her *now*. You daren't take any risks.'

Relieved to have her own opinion confirmed, Laura went to the phone and was pleased to get a quick reply. At least she hadn't disturbed Sister's sleep. 'I'll come immediately, Nurse, and I hope I shall find you've got everything ready.'

When she arrived she looked just as usual, so evidently the rest had done her good. Half an hour later Penny's little son was born.

'You'll let Adrian know, won't you?' the new mother begged, looking up at Laura over her baby's tuft of gingerish hair. 'Tell him to come and see me this evening.'

Sister made no comment but afterwards she came into the nursery where Laura was attending to the new arrival's first toilet. 'Is Adrian the child's father?' she asked.

'Er—no. He's the man Penny says she's going to marry.'

'These young people. . .!' She sighed heavily. 'I'm afraid I shall never understand them, Nurse, but perhaps it's easier for you, being nearer their age. You'd better go and ring up this man as soon as you've finished here, and I hope to goodness there won't be any complications.'

But Sister's hopes were not to be realised.

'Can I see Penny Johnson, please?'

Laura looked up at the tall young man with tow-coloured longish hair who had appeared at the nurses' station. Was this Adrian or Dave? He had a pleasant, if rather anxious expression and she liked him instinctively, so she hoped very much he was the right one.

'Visiting time hasn't started yet but fathers are allowed——' Laura broke off in dismay. Adrian *wasn't* a father. But surely, under the circumstances, he could be accorded the same privileges?

But supposing he was Dave? He might have managed to find out about the birth even though he hadn't been officially told, and Penny had seemed to be really scared that he might turn up.

'May I have your name?' she asked briskly.

'Adrian Williams. She'll be expecting me.'

Greatly relieved, Laura took him to the three-bedded room where Penny had been allotted a bed. Her baby was in a perspex cot at her side and she was gazing at him adoringly. The arrival of Adrian seemed to put a seal on her happiness and Laura left them holding hands and gazing into each other's eyes.

'Very touching,' Sister observed quietly when she saw them. 'It's a pity he's the wrong man.'

Laura didn't think he was. Without knowing anything about Dave, let alone meeting him, she had taken an instinctive dislike to him.

The following evening she had her opinion confirmed.

It had been a busy day and the nurses were all looking forward to going off duty. In addition, there had been a difficult birth which had necessitated Martin's being called in, and he was still in the ward when the uproar started. There were uplifted voices and one in particular—a man's—was shouting incoherently.

'What on earth——?' Martin set off in the direction of the noise at a fast pace which was not quite a run.

Laura followed him closely, passing Sister, who had only just come out of her office, and making for the room where Penny had her bed. As she reached the doorway she was horrified to see that the girl now had two male visitors.

The newcomer was shorter and stockier than Adrian, with sandy hair and vivid blue eyes. He stood nearest to the cot, facing the other man belligerently. 'This kid's mine—see? I was willing to marry Penny and she wouldn't have me. Well, she's not going to marry you either—you've got no right to take my child and bring it up like it was yours——'

The other two mothers were watching in alarm. They both had their husbands with them but neither man seemed inclined to intervene. As Laura stood frozen in the doorway, Martin took a step forward.

'Calm down, for God's sake.' His voice was quiet and very firm. 'We can't allow you to upset the whole ward like this. Come out to the waiting-room and talk this over privately.'

'Like hell I will!' Dave snarled. 'What's it got to do with you anyway? Get out of my way!' He acted so swiftly that, although Martin lunged forward, he somehow managed to elude him. The baby's cot was on the side of the bed nearest to the door, and in a split second it was snatched up with one arm while the other fist slammed into Martin's face.

But it was Laura who caught the full brunt of Dave's fury. She tried to hold her position blocking the doorway but found herself flung aside as though she weighed nothing. Reeling back helplessly, she fell with a crash to the floor, hitting her head on the corner of Penny's locker on the way down.

She saw nothing of the frantic pursuit. When she opened her eyes a few seconds later there was complete silence—or what seemed like silence after the preceding noise. But, as Sister's face swam into view above, she suddenly realised that someone was sobbing heartbrokenly in the background.

'You seem to have had rather a nasty knock, Nurse Marsden,' said the calm, flat voice. 'You'd better lie down in the labour-room for a while.'

'I'm all right.' Laura sat up and tried to pretend she wasn't feeling horribly dizzy. 'Is that Penny crying? She must be in a terrible state.'

'No doubt, after the disgraceful scene which has just taken place, but I think you can safely leave her to me. As soon as Mr Kent comes back I'll get him to authorise a sedative.'

'Yes, Sister,' Laura said meekly and allowed herself to be helped to her feet. The dizziness was passing though she still felt very odd, but her concern for Penny was so great that she didn't think she could possibly withdraw from the ward and lie down. 'I really don't need——' she began.

'You'll do as I say, Nurse.'

Rebelliously, but knowing argument to be useless, Laura went off to the labour-room and stretched out on the bed. And it was there that Jenny found her a short time later.

'I came out of the locker-room to see what on earth was happening and Sister sent me to see if you were all right. Are you?'

'Of course I am.' Laura swung her legs to the floor. 'Oh, Jenny—it was terrible! That poor baby! Do you think they've caught Dave?'

'Is that who it was? I should think they've caught him by now. He didn't have much of a start.' Jenny's eyes gleamed with excitement. 'What an incredible drama for Cecilia! I'm sure nothing like it has ever happened before.'

'It wasn't funny,' Laura said reproachfully.

'I'm sure it wasn't, but it must have been rather thrilling to be right in the middle of it.'

Laura rubbed her aching head and made no comment, and at that moment the door opened again and Martin came in.

'Sister said you were lying down so I don't know why you're sitting like that. Lie down again at once.' And to Jenny he added, 'Put a blanket over her. She shouldn't be allowed to get cold after a shock like that.'

'Never mind the shock *I* had!' Laura remained sitting up in spite of Martin's instructions. 'What happened? Did you get the baby back?'

'Yes, of course—what do you suppose? That guy hadn't a chance of making a complete get-away.' He smiled. 'The infant was still sleeping peacefully, believe it or not. I reckon he thought he was back in the uterus and his mum was being unusually energetic.'

'Oh, thank goodness! I'm so relieved—I was so worried—and—and dreadfully sorry for Penny.' She was incoherent as a great burden of fear seemed to roll away from her and at the same time reaction set in, her eyes filled with tears and she began to shake uncontrollably.

Martin put a hand on her shoulder and firmly pressed her down into a prone position. 'Will you please do as you're told? Where's that blanket, Jenny?'

'I don't want a blanket—I'm off duty soon and then I'm going home——'

'Stop behaving like an idiot,' Martin ordered her. 'You know perfectly well you should rest after a bang on the head. How's it feeling?' He examined the bump with gentle fingers.

Laura winced at his touch and tried to hide it. 'I can rest when I get home,' she protested.

He shook his head over her. 'You surely don't imagine I'm going to let you drive yourself back to Mayes?'

'Why not? I'm p-perfectly capable of doing so.' She was still shaking, and as Jenny advanced on her with a blanket she suddenly subsided meekly.

Her head really was aching rather badly and it was lovely to lie still and do nothing. But abruptly she remembered something. 'You got hurt too, didn't you? That awful Dave——'

'Did me no harm at all. I turned my head and

the blow glanced off. All that happened was that it prevented me from grabbing him before he started his getaway.' He looked at his watch. 'I'll be back for you in twenty minutes, Laura. You can leave your car here overnight and I'll give you a lift in the morning if you're well enough to work.'

When the door had closed behind him, Jenny pulled a face. 'You weren't very appreciative of his tender loving care,' she commented. 'Is it because you don't like being bossed around? Or have you started disliking him again?'

But Laura closed her eyes and made no reply. She couldn't avoid giving Martin's care of her full marks, but she didn't believe it was either tender or loving. No doubt those kind of feelings were reserved for Lucy.

CHAPTER EIGHT

MARTIN returned punctually, again felt Laura's head and gave his permission for her to get up.

'Take it easy,' he advised as they went down the corridor and got into the lift. Two nurses who were sharing it with them looked at her curiously and Laura felt ridiculous. There was nothing the matter with her now that she had got over the shock of Dave's attack. She didn't need all this cosseting.

As they walked to the car park she suddenly remembered that she wasn't on duty the next day until two o'clock, so she could have a lazy morning. The prospect was pleasing until it also occurred to her she would need her car for getting to the hospital. And that meant driving herself home now.

'Certainly not!' Martin exclaimed when she had laboriously explained it to him. 'You know as well as I do that nobody should drive a car when they've had a bad knock on the head. Assuming that you're fit to work tomorrow afternoon, isn't there a bus?'

'I believe so but I don't think it's very convenient.'

'I'll ask Lucy to give you a lift into Wickenfield. She can easily fit it in with some shopping.' He unlocked his car door and ushered her in with the air of a man who had solved a tiresome problem and wanted no further argument.

But Laura persisted. 'I really couldn't possibly bother her——'

'Since she still believes herself to be in your debt over the way you helped when Lorraine was hurrying into the world, she'll be only too glad to drive you.' He got in and slammed the door. 'So that's settled.'

Laura was too tired to discuss it any more, and it would certainly have been a waste of time anyway. Neither of them spoke during the short drive to the village, but there was time for thinking and Laura's thoughts were dominated by Lucy Goring. No doubt she would agree to give her a lift into Wickenfield, since Martin would have told her she must. She had a gentle, pliable nature and probably enjoyed being ordered about by a man who was obviously extremely important in her life. Just *how* important the relationship was Laura was not prepared to put into words even in her own mind. She would know for sure one day and until then she must try not to think about it.

Outside Lavender Cottage Martin demanded her key and let her into the house. It was dusk and he went ahead, switching on lights and instructing her to make herself a hot drink and then go to bed. 'I'll call in tomorrow morning,' he said, standing in the porch and looking back, 'just to make sure you're OK for work.'

'Thank you,' Laura murmured meekly, but when the door closed she went straight to the kitchen and cut herself a thick slice of bread and cheese. It didn't seem to have occurred to him that she had had no supper. Or did he consider starvation to be the best treatment for shock?

Her brave attempt at a joke was short-lived and she was suddenly overwhelmed by depression. Fighting tears, she toiled upstairs and crawled into bed. But it was a long time before she slept. Over and over again she lived through Dave's frantic snatching of the cot with the sleeping baby in it, her own attempt to stop him and subsequent brief spell of unconsciousness, the horror of coming round and not knowing whether the baby was safe or not.

It was eight o'clock when she woke the next morning and she got up quickly and put on her blue velvet caftan. Looking in the mirror as she brushed her silky hair, she was pleased to see that her colour had come back, and if she arranged her hair carefully the bruise would be hidden. She was just finishing a hearty breakfast when Martin arrived.

'How are you feeling?' He came briskly in, ran his eye over her and seemed pleased with what he saw.

'I'm fine,' she said, smiling.

'Headache?'

'None at all.'

'Then I think we can assume you're fit to go on duty at two o'clock.'

Laura had already assumed it but she restrained herself from saying so. 'What time will Lucy call for me?' she asked.

'I told her about one-thirty. She said to tell you she was very glad to help.'

They were standing close to each other by the kitchen table, and suddenly the atmosphere was full of tension. Afraid that he would notice the quickening of her breathing, Laura tried to back away but the table was behind her. The deadpan expression which so often hid his feelings was gone. Tenderness looked at her out of his eyes and round his mouth there was an unaccountable sadness. 'Don't do it again, Laura,' he said gently. 'It's never a good idea to tangle with someone like Dave. Next time you might get really hurt.'

Somehow she managed to laugh. 'There's not likely to be a next time! We don't go in for that sort of drama in Cecilia, thank goodness!'

When he had gone, she sat down again rather suddenly because her legs were trembling. Maybe she hadn't recovered as much as she thought?

She spent the morning proving to herself she was fit by doing some weeding. By the time Lucy called for her she had managed to convince herself that the incident by the kitchen table had been grossly exaggerated by her imagination.

Lucy looked attractive in blue cotton trousers

and an Indian cotton jumper. She proved compe-
tent at the wheel and they chatted all the way into
town.

'I'm glad to have this opportunity of talking to
you,' she said when she had commented on
Laura's adventure and answered questions regarding her baby's progress. 'I have a suggestion to
make.'

Laura remembered that Martin had told her
about Lucy wanting to give a party but it turned
out to be something quite different.

'It was dark that evening you came to my house
so perhaps you didn't notice I have a swimming-
pool. It's quite a big one and heated too so it's
usable when the weather isn't all that good. I
wondered if you and your friends would like to
take advantage of it. It really doesn't get much
use, though Martin swims there most mornings.
My boys are too young and I don't have all that
much time. I hate to think of it being wasted, so it
really would be a kindness if you could rustle up
some people to enjoy it.'

'I'm sure I could do that,' Laura said warmly.
'I'm only an ordinary sort of swimmer myself, but
Anita is magnificent and Jenny's quite good.'

'What about the boys?'

'I honestly don't know and, of course, house
surgeons get very little time, but I'll certainly tell
them about your offer.'

She added rather fulsome thanks which Lucy
brushed aside, and then they were at the hospital.

Making the round which she always liked to

find time for if possible when she came on duty, Laura found Penny calm but subdued. She had been moved to a different bed and the cot was as far from the door as possible. Later, finding Jenny in the sluice, she discussed the incident briefly. 'What do you think will happen to Dave?' she asked.

'Sister said he'd been reported to the police but I reckon he'll get off with a warning, seeing as how he didn't succeed in kidnapping the baby. I expect they'll keep an eye on him though.'

'The sooner Penny marries Adrian the better. Then she'll have someone to look after her.' She suddenly remembered Lucy's suggestion and told Jenny about it.

'Super! I don't expect we'll be able to take advantage of it much though because of the difficulty in getting there. We haven't *all* got a car!'

Laura threw a packet of disposable nappies at her, after which they returned soberly to the ward.

After the excitement of yesterday, things seemed strangely quiet. There were no women in labour and none expected, though no one could ever take it for granted that some impatient infant wouldn't decide to make an early appearance.

'This doesn't seem right,' the midwife on duty commented as she and Laura met in the kitchen, each intent on purloining a cup of the patients' tea.

Laura didn't ask what she meant. 'You're surely not complaining because we're not busy?' she exclaimed. 'We get plenty of days when we don't know whether we're coming or going.'

'I wasn't exactly complaining, and I don't suppose the calm will last long enough for us to get really bored.' The midwife glanced at Laura as she sat at the table sipping her tea. 'You look a bit cheesed off yourself. Is your head still hurting?'

'Oh, no—so long as I don't touch it.' Laura glanced at the window and improvised rapidly. 'I expect it's the weather—it feels a bit like thunder.' She hadn't noticed it that morning, but during the afternoon clouds had rolled up and now hung heavy and threatening over the hospital.

'Sister was saying how airless it seems.' The midwife drained her cup and grimaced. 'This tea really is terrible! I don't know how the patients stand it.'

'They get it before it's stewed,' Laura pointed out. She sipped her own and then went on diffidently, 'It's not like Sister to complain about the weather. She usually takes all sorts in her stride.'

'She's not taking anything in her stride just now. Do you know she actually admitted to me the other day that she was looking forward to retirement?'

'You think she's ill?'

'I wouldn't go that far, but she isn't well either. It's my belief she's a martyr to indigestion and that could be due to eating all the wrong food. She's so old-fashioned that she probably considers modern ideas about diet a load of rubbish.'

'I hope you're right.'

But two hours later, just as they were preparing to serve supper, the midwife was proved wrong.

The meals trolley had arrived from the kitchen, propelled by an orderly. Sister was at the nurses' station as it passed, scolding the most junior of the student nurses for some trivial offence. 'Get on with serving supper now, Nurse,' she ordered, 'and do try to keep your mind on what you're doing. It's most important that you——' She broke off abruptly and pressed her hand against her diaphragm.

At that moment Laura came out of one of the rooms. The student grimaced at her and went off to do as she had been told, but Laura scarcely noticed. Her eyes were on Sister as she walked rapidly towards the office. Why was she moving in such a strange way, almost as though she wanted to double up?

All her instincts were urging her to go in pursuit, yet she still hesitated. Sister wouldn't thank her if she'd had a spasm of indigestion, and even to offer a dose of magnesia wouldn't be welcome.

Laura's mind was abruptly made up. If she got her head bitten off it would be just too bad but she wouldn't let it worry her. She simply *had* to find out what was wrong.

The door was closed but she knocked and then bravely opened it without being told to come in. One glance confirmed that she had been right to investigate. Sister was slumped over the desk, her face ashen and beads of sweat on her forehead. She saw Laura and said faintly, 'I'm afraid I shall have to go off duty. The pain——' But the sentence was never finished. With a groan she slid to the floor and lay there in a heap as unconsciousness mercifully put an end to the agony.

Laura took one horrified look and leapt to the phone. But before she could lift the receiver she heard the swish of the swing doors leading to the corridor and paused for a second. Martin sometimes called in during the early evening though she didn't think it could be him now, since there was so little happening in the ward.

It *was* Martin. He said casually, 'I just looked in to make sure everything was OK——' He broke off abruptly, his grey eyes suddenly keen and searching. 'What on earth's the matter, Laura?'

'Come and look.' She stepped to one side so he could see into the office.

'Good God!' He went down on his knees and felt the pulse beating in the carotid artery. 'Scarcely perceptible,' he reported a moment later. 'How long has she been out cold like this?'

'Less than a minute. I was just going to phone.'

'I'll do it. We must get her out of here as soon as possible.' Martin stood up and barked his orders into the receiver.

As they waited for the porter with a trolley, Laura said diffidently, 'Have you any idea what's wrong? I know it's a silly question but. . .' Her voice died away.

She expected him to say sarcastically, 'If it's a silly question, why ask it?' but instead of that he looked down at her gravely.

'Have you any suggestions to make? You see more of her than I do.'

'Internal haemorrhage?'

'Very likely. I've suspected for some time that she might have an ulcer, and it's my guess it's perforated. I'm afraid she's very ill indeed.'

'You'd think she'd know she needed treatment. We were all worried about her.'

'Of course she knew, but she probably hoped to struggle on until her retirement. After all, medical people are notorious for not looking after their own health.'

They lapsed into silence as they heard the approach of the trolley. With great care, Martin and the porter lifted the unconscious woman and covered her warmly with the red blanket.

'There's nothing special you want me for in the ward?' he asked.

Laura shook her head. 'But you'll come back and tell us about Sister?'

'If I can, but it may not be for some time.'

When they had gone, Laura sought out the midwife since she would obviously have to take charge for the time being.

'How extraordinary that it should happen so soon after our conversation!' she exclaimed when she had been put in the picture. 'Poor Sister Leggett—it seems an awful shame and yet it's her

own fault, the silly woman. You'd think she would
have had more sense! I suppose she's been trying
to treat herself medically when she was urgently
needing surgery.'

'I wonder who we'll get in her place?' Laura
said. 'Perhaps they'll make you acting sister, since
you're the senior midwife. Would you mind?'

The middle-aged woman, not far from retirement herself, shook her grey head. 'Not so long as
it was really only acting. I'm not ambitious in that
way. I just want to go on delivering babies because
that's what I enjoy. You have to do a lot of other
things as well if you're a sister.'

They were not surprised to get a visit from a
senior nursing officer before long, a brisk and
businesslike woman who did exactly what had
been anticipated. When asked for news of Sister
she pursed her lips and looked disapproving.
'There's not much I can tell you. She's going to
theatres later on, but at present she's being treated
for shock in the Sick Bay. No visitors, of course.'

'As though we'd even *think* of going to see her!'
Laura exclaimed indignantly when she had gone.
'Does she imagine we're morons?'

'Probably.' The midwife smiled. 'The visitors
will be here soon, Laura. Hadn't you better make
sure there are no babies requiring feeding first?'

The gentle reminder galvanised Laura into
action and she sped off to make sure the supper
dishes had all been cleared away. It seemed both
an age and yet no time at all since the supper

trolley had arrived and Sister had still been standing at the nurses' station. And now she was hospitalised herself and was to have an emergency operation. The peaceful day was rapidly becoming far too dramatic.

Things continued to happen. A and E phoned to say they had a patient for admission, brought to the hospital by ambulance. She had left home in rapid labour and become a mother on the way, her child skilfully delivered by the ambulance attendant. After that no one was surprised when two women arrived almost together, both about to start the second stage of labour.

Since Martin was still on the premises, he came up with Jonathan to see the first arrival and spent some time with her, making sure that the placenta had come away intact and then checking the baby over very carefully. 'It's not usually a good thing to be so precipitate,' he said to Laura, touching the downy head gently with a long finger, 'but this little girl seems to have taken it in her stride.'

'So did Lucy's,' Laura pointed out.

'Granted; but I'm still not recommending it.' He moved away from the cot and lowered his voice. 'I expect you've had news of Sister by now?'

'Yes, thank you. Miss Hetherington came up and told us.' She was feeling quite ridiculously wooden and angry with herself because of it. As she allowed an exasperated sigh to escape her, Martin's gaze became keener.

'Has all the excitement been too much for you after what happened yesterday?'

'Of course not!' She was pink with indignation. 'I've never liked this heavy thundery weather. When I get home I shall take myself for a good walk and breathe in some fresher air than we get here.'

He raised one eyebrow with what seemed to her maddening superiority. 'Perhaps it's escaped your notice that it's pouring with rain?'

'What?' Laura swung round to look out of the window. 'So it is—what a nuisance!'

'There's nothing to prevent you having your walk provided you've got suitable clothing and an umbrella,' he pointed out. 'It will be all the more refreshing for being wet.'

Why on earth were they having this absurd conversation? Compelled to continue it, Laura raised her chin and returned his amused stare. 'I have both, thank you.'

'Good.' The twinkle became a smile. 'So there'll be no need at all for me to feel uncomfortable if I pass you splashing through the puddles round the green. I shall know that any offer of a lift would be most unwelcome.'

Laura flushed and could think of no suitable retort. She was glad when he left the nursery and she could force her mind to concentrate on what she was doing. By the time she went off duty the rain had become a mere drizzle, but she felt no enthusiasm for the walk she had pretended to be so keen about. Without any difficulty at all she abandoned the whole idea.

Ahead of her lay a gloriously peaceful evening, or so she imagined, but she had only been at home long enough to change into trousers and a shirt when the doorbell rang.

It was unlikely to be a neighbour for, although they had seemed friendly at first, Laura had sensed a certain reserve in them since her house-warming party. Nobody had actually complained but she felt pretty sure someone would if it happened again.

And it was even more unlikely to be Martin.

Nevertheless, Laura's heartbeats quickened as she went to open the door and when she saw who stood there the pace speeded up alarmingly. It wasn't anyone she knew. It was a policeman.

He looked very large and official and she was suddenly full of apprehension. Why had he come? It couldn't be anything to do with the car, and her conscience in other matters was equally clear. Or was it?

'Mind if I come in, miss?' he asked politely. 'There's something I want to check up on.'

'Of course I don't mind, but I don't know how I can help you.' Laura held the door wider to allow the passage of his large frame. 'Come and sit down.'

'It won't take long.' The officer settled himself in one of the armchairs, completely filling it. 'You'll recall making a statement to the police about that

accident on the pedestrian crossing involving Mr
Martin Kent and Nurse Sally Milne?'

'Yes, of course.' Laura's hands began to twist
together nervously and she hurriedly relaxed
them. 'What about it?'

'I was wondering if maybe you'd like to amend
it?'

This was it, the point of no return. She could
explain that, on second thoughts, she had realised
how very little she had actually seen, apologise for
the error and make a new statement. Or she could
stick firmly to what she had said originally.

Playing for time, she asked, 'Why should I want
to do that?'

'Because the young lady, who has now quite
recovered from her concussion, is stating that the
doctor started off before the green light for traffic
and knocked her down while she still had priority.'

'But that's ridiculous!' Glad that on this point
she could be absolutely truthful, Laura went rushing on. 'As a matter of fact I was among the last to
get across during the flashing amber light. Anybody behind me must have crossed—or tried to—
after the lights changed. I'm sure Nurse Milne
believes what she told you, but the fact remains
that concussion can have very strange effects and
she doesn't realise she's got it wrong.'

'Hmm.' The policeman produced a statement
form and studied it. 'It says here you told the
police at the scene of the accident that you actually
saw what took place. Are you prepared to endorse
that now?'

Laura drew a deep breath. 'Yes—yes, I am,' she said firmly.

'Very well, miss. That seems to settle the matter, since it agrees with the doctor's own statement. The young lady thought we ought to make a case of it but there are no grounds for that apart from what she herself has told us—which is entirely uncorroborated.' He folded his papers and stood up. 'I won't take up any more of your time, and thank you for your co-operation.'

Laura saw him off with a sigh of relief. So it was over. Martin wouldn't get into trouble for something which was no fault of his, and she wouldn't either have to let him down in court or commit perjury. Perjury was a horrible-sounding word and she shied away from it. She had no feeling of having done wrong even though she was technically at fault. In fact, she didn't see how she could have acted in any other way.

That settled satisfactorily, she went along to the kitchen to make herself some coffee when the doorbell rang again. And this time it *was* Martin.

Immediately it struck her he was looking exceedingly serious. He said quietly, 'If you're not too busy I would like a word with you.'

'I'm not busy. I—I was just going to have some coffee and then get supper. Would you like some?'

'Not just now, thank you.' He followed her into the sitting-room but did not sit down. 'I've just had a visit from a policeman,' he stated baldly.

'Have you?' Laura tried to speak naturally. 'So have I.'

'I know. I stopped to post a letter and saw him coming away. He recognised me and paused to let me know I have you to thank for getting me off the hook regarding that accident. At least, he didn't put it quite like that but his meaning was obvious.'

Until then Laura had had an unpleasant feeling of being caught off balance. But an unexpected spurt of anger came to her rescue.

'You don't *have* to thank me,' she blazed. 'It's quite clear it's nearly choking you so I shouldn't bother if I were you.'

The attack seemed to surprise him. He raised his eyebrows and drawled, 'You have a very curious idea of my emotions, Laura. I have no problem whatsoever about thanking people when I feel the thanks are justified, but I don't at all care for the notion that someone is lying on my behalf. If you really had seen anything I would have been very grateful for your support, but you couldn't possibly have witnessed the accident——'

'So what? You're only splitting hairs. We both know Sally was entirely to blame.' Laura tilted her head back and met his eyes defiantly.

It was because she was looking at him so intently that she saw his expression change. They had been standing in the middle of the room, facing each other like two boxers, but now Martin took a step forward and put his hands on her shoulders. 'Shall we regard this unfortunate incident as now closed? And will you believe that I'm grateful in spite of all I've said?'

'I—I don't find that very easy,' she faltered.

'Then let's make our peace by having supper together. I've got some steak in my fridge and it's far too big for one. I'd like it very much if you'd come along to the flat and share it.'

Laura gasped. The suddenness of the invitation had plunged her mind into a whirl and she did not know how to answer him. They had been fighting each other only a moment ago and now he was proposing a friendly meal together. Yet if she refused he might think she was still annoyed at his apparent lack of gratitude.

'Oh—er—thank you. I haven't tasted steak for quite a long time,' she heard herself saying woodenly.

'That's settled, then.' He was on his way to the door. 'I'll go and start preparations. See you!'

When he had gone, Laura stood for a moment in a trance of disbelief. Had she really committed herself to sharing his supper? The absurdity of it almost made her burst out laughing, but it would have been hysterical laughter rather than genuine amusement.

With an effort she pulled herself together. She'd better change again—and be quick about it too or he'd want to know why she was late!

She went to her bedroom and began to undo

buttons with hands which shook. What with Sister's collapse, the policeman's visit and now this, the day was being very nearly too much for her.

And there was more to come too.

CHAPTER NINE

LAURA felt better when she had put on a blue cord skirt and Grecian-type tunic with heavy embroidery. She brushed her neat cap of blonde hair, made up her eyes to tone with her outfit and added a touch of lipstick. Her cheeks, she observed critically, were remarkably pink but perhaps that was the aftermath of the quarrel.

It certainly couldn't be nervous excitement because she was going to supper with a man she detested.

Walking to Hill House, she suddenly wondered whether the granny flat had its own front door. The thought of explaining herself to Lucy was embarrassing, and she ventured round the side of the house. The swimming-pool immediately caught her eye and it was, as its owner had said, a very nice one. Facing it, to her relief, she discovered a neat cream painted front door with 'Hill House Flat' in wrought-iron letters on a small board.

The man who opened the door was a Martin she had never seen. He wore lightweight fawn trousers and a maroon polo-necked sweater, both protected by a shiny plastic apron adorned with pictures of herbs. He said tersely, 'Be with you in

a moment. Sit down and make yourself at home,'
and disappeared into the kitchen.

'Can't I help?' Laura asked.

'No, you can't. I'm quite a good cook but I like
to do it by myself.'

'Fair enough,' she said lightly, and found her
way into the sitting-room.

Ignoring his instructions about sitting down, she
began to wander about the large room. It was
furnished rather elegantly with a strange mixture
of articles. There was an antique bureau and a very
modern music-centre. Plain, functional book-
shelves crowded with books occupied most of one
wall, and a Victorian needlework table looked as
though it belonged in a lady's boudoir. The brown
leather armchairs were thoroughly masculine and
would have been at home in a London club. On
the wall opposite the books a vividly coloured and
quite incomprehensible painting made a splash of
brightness in a rather sombre room.

On the small table there was a photograph of a
wedding group, but when Laura carried it to the
window she discovered that the bride and groom
were missing; and yet the occasion was definitely
a wedding because there were unmistakable
bridesmaids among the guests. She was puzzling
over it when she heard a voice behind her.

'I see you're studying a photograph taken at
Lucy's wedding.' Martin put down the bowl of
salad he was carrying and came to stand at her
shoulder. 'I took it myself actually and had it

enlarged because it has my parents on it. It was a stroke of luck that I didn't include the bridal pair in this one because I could hardly keep it on that table now that the marriage has collapsed.'

Laura stared at the tall man with grey hair and broad shoulders, and the slender woman with Martin's clear-cut features who was wearing a smart black and white outfit. She was holding herself very upright and looked as though she would stand no nonsense from anybody. Something else inherited by her son.

'They were both killed in a car crash not long after.' Martin's voice was flat and unemotional but Laura sensed an underlying tension. 'Lucy's parents were with them and her father was killed too. The two families have always been close and, naturally, the accident tightened the bonds between them.'

'I can understand that,' Laura said quietly.

The information was interesting and explained why Lucy and Martin seemed to know each other so very well. But it did not answer the important question dominating Laura's thoughts. What was the present relationship between them?

'How do you like your steak?' Martin was asking.

'Medium, if you don't mind.'

'Of course I don't mind! You're my guest and naturally I want you to have it as you like it.'

Good manners were really wasted on him, Laura

reflected. And yet he could be as formally courteous as anyone when he liked. The trouble was that you couldn't ever be sure which approach would be more acceptable at any particular moment in time.

She left the window and returned the photograph to its place. The gloomy sky was making the room very dark and, before he had gone back to the kitchen, Martin had switched on two table-lamps, immediately creating an atmosphere of warmth and comfort.

Before long he reappeared minus the apron and put down two small bowls on the dining-table.

'Avocado pear for starters, with cottage cheese and prawns,' he announced. 'OK?'

'Very much so.' Laura joined him with alacrity and gazed admiringly at the beautifully presented first course. 'If you hadn't gone in for medicine you could have been a chef.'

'No, I couldn't. I only practise the culinary art as an antidote to medicine. I'm sure you'll agree that there are times when you badly need one.'

Were they going to argue all through the meal? she wondered, and was relieved to find this was not the case. Martin suddenly switched the conversation to what appeared to be his other interest—classical jazz.

'I've got a new record I'd like you to hear—and if you tell me you'd rather have pop, I shan't ever cook you a meal again.'

Luckily she was able to reassure him on this

point, and as she did so it occurred to her she was unlikely to be invited again in any case. This surely had to be a one-off occasion.

When they had eaten she was allowed to help clear the table but not to wash up, since he assured her that this would be done in the morning by his cleaning lady. The meal had been so beautifully served that she was astonished to find the small kitchen looking as though half a dozen very untidy cooks had worked there.

'Somehow I expected it to be clinically neat!' she exclaimed.

'You think that would fit my personality?' Martin piled dishes in the sink and ran water over them.

They had drunk a bottle of wine with their meal and perhaps that was why Laura felt emboldened to say, 'I wouldn't have thought you would be able to tolerate a muddle like that.' She paused and then added rashly, 'You're so very intolerant at the hospital if people don't come up to your standards.'

'And why shouldn't I be? I expect a high standard from myself.'

'But everybody isn't as clever as you. It's harder for them.'

She had expected an explosion but he appeared to be thinking about what she had said. The long dark lashes hid his eyes and she could not guess at his thoughts, so that when he finally spoke his comment surprised her.

'I don't think I like this bloke you've been describing. Is it really meant to be me?'

Laura immediately found herself apologising wildly. 'I'm sorry—I should never have been so outspoken. Please forget all about it.'

'I shall do nothing of the sort.' He grinned suddenly. 'I shall have the words "Do not be intolerant" framed and hung above my bed like those texts our great-grandparents went in for.' He led the way back to the sitting-room. 'And now you've finished analysing my character, let's have some music while we drink our coffee.'

They sat decorously on the settee, to all appearances giving their full attention to the wailing saxophones. At first Laura could not forget her appallingly plain speaking in the kitchen, but gradually she relaxed. She hadn't said anything which wasn't true and consultants didn't get much of that. Maybe it would do him good.

The pleasant, comfortable room, now lit by only one lamp, was full of shadows. The brooding outside world, hushed in anticipation of a storm, made no impact, and she had a feeling that she and Martin were alone in a small isolated world of their own. It was a long, long time since she had been so happy.

She had no right to feel like that. The happiness was only borrowed and the sea of physical well-being on which she floated was only temporary, but somehow Laura managed to thrust that unwelcome reminder to the back of her mind. It lurked there, for the moment defeated, but biding its time.

The music ended and in the ensuing silence they heard the rumble of thunder. A jagged streak of lightning flashed across the sky and briefly lighted up the room. Martin got up and pulled the curtains across, and when he returned to the settee he sat down much closer to Laura. She could feel his warmth and the weight of his shoulder against hers.

When he put his arm round her she allowed her head to rest against him. He rubbed his cheek over the smoothness of her hair and murmured something, but she was in such a state of intoxication that she did not hear what he said. It was as though her mind was numb while her whole body clamoured for attention, making its needs known with a desperation which would have frightened her if she had been capable of cogent thought.

Martin moved suddenly, his mouth seeking hers, and she surrendered eagerly, shameless in the urgency of her desire.

At that moment the telephone rang.

'Hell!' He leapt to his feet and Laura fell back against the settee, her breath still coming quickly as she struggled to get a grip on herself.

Her bemused mind had come back to life and was demanding to know what on earth she thought she was up to, letting herself get carried away like that. She should have been prepared for it and therefore better able to cope. A man didn't invite a girl to have supper alone with him in his flat without taking it for granted that there would be some sort of romantic dalliance afterwards— meaningless but enjoyable at the time.

Act your age, Laura, she admonished herself, and willed her pounding heart to slow down.

Martin's conversation on the phone was brief. She heard him say, 'OK—I'll be there in a few minutes,' and then he turned to face her. 'Sorry to have to put an end to this very pleasant interlude. I've got to return to the hospital pronto. Emergency Caesarean.'

Laura stood up at once, now fully in control. 'I ought to be going anyway. It's getting late. Thanks for the heavenly meal, Martin, and—and the concert. I hope you won't find anything really serious awaiting you.'

'If it hadn't been serious they wouldn't have sent for me,' he pointed out impatiently.

Things were back to normal.

The weather in the morning matched Laura's mood. The thunder had done nothing to clear the air and it still rained intermittently, continuing like that all day.

Determined to rise above her unhappiness, she plunged into work and succeeded in banishing it at least for the time being. She even succeeded in hiding from Jenny the fact that she had a very great deal on her mind, but perhaps that was because Jenny was worried about Anita.

'She seems dreadfully depressed. If I can get her to come to my room for coffee tonight, will you come as well? We haven't been together, the three of us, for ages.'

'Of course I'll come,' Laura said, 'but I'm not likely to be any more successful than you in cheering Anita up.'

'I didn't mean that exactly. I just thought it would be nice to sit and talk like we used to before you went up-market.'

'I'm not up-market! Just because I was lucky enough to be left a cottage doesn't mean *I'm* any different. Anyway, I sometimes find it rather lonely and occasionally I even miss the nurses' home.'

Jenny laughed disbelievingly and they parted.

They were both on duty until eight o'clock and they walked across to the nurses' home together. There was no sign of Anita and they had just decided to have their own coffee without waiting any longer when there was a tap on the door and she came in.

Anita's skin had lost its glow of health and she looked utterly weary. Without a word she collapsed into a chair and leaned back, apparently neither noticing nor caring that her friends were staring at her in concern.

'Are you OK?' Laura asked anxiously. 'You look just about all in.'

Anita made an effort to sit upright. 'I do feel a

bit tired. I came off duty at five o'clock and went for a long walk.'

'In the rain?' Jenny exclaimed. 'I thought you hated wet weather.'

Concerned as she was at the girl's shattered appearance, Laura's wayward mind flew back to yesterday when she had had a conversation with Martin about walking in the rain. When she returned to the present, Anita was describing how she had tramped down to the river—quite a distance from the hospital—and wandered along the tow path for a while.

'Very depressing, I should think, on a night like this,' Jenny scolded her. 'And it's lonely too. You might have been mugged, or raped or even murdered. It really was a crazy thing to do and not a bit like you.'

There was a brief silence and then Anita said defiantly, 'Perhaps I felt crazy.'

The other two exchanged alarmed glances. 'Are we allowed to ask what that's supposed to mean?' Laura enquired.

They waited anxiously while Anita struggled with a visible reluctance. Eventually she burst out, 'You'll have to know soon so I might as well tell you now. I'm pregnant and—and—oh, God——' she hid her face in her hands '—I've been so dreadfully worried because I didn't know what to do!'

Afterwards Jenny and Laura agreed that they ought to have suspected it. Anita hadn't been herself for some time but they had put it down to the usual pressure of work, and not delved any further. Consequently, at the moment of impact, the news was a considerable shock.

'How far have you got?' Jenny asked.

'I've only missed once but I had a test and it was positive.'

'No wonder you haven't been yourself lately. Why didn't you tell us before?'

'I wanted to get used to it first, but——' her voice quivered '——I haven't been very successful.'

'Gavin knows?' Laura asked.

'Yes. That was why I had to go for a long walk. I wanted to do some uninterrupted thinking. He wants us to get married.'

'So what are you worrying about, then? You love each other so it wouldn't really be a shotgun wedding.'

Anita took a deep breath and her voice strengthened. 'But we're not going to get married.'

'*Not*? What are you going to do then?'

Anita ignored Jenny's question and went on speaking as though she had not heard it. 'I won't let Gavin marry me just because we've been careless and started a baby. He's right at the beginning of his medical career and it would be crazy to tie himself down with a wife and child.'

'It's been done before.'

'That doesn't make it right.'

Neither of her friends attempted to continue the

argument. The responsibility of advocating marriage under such circumstances would be too great.

'You've got two alternatives,' Laura said. 'You can either have the baby and cope all by yourself, or you can ask for a termination.'

'I wouldn't be quite alone. I don't think my family would cast me off though I know they'd be shocked. We were all very strictly brought up.'

'But would they be prepared to look after the child while you returned to work? There'd be all sorts of problems.'

Anita made an impatient gesture. 'Do you think I don't know that? I've been over it again and again.'

'That leaves abortion,' Jenny stated bluntly. 'I don't know how you feel about that. Some people have very strong opinions on the subject.'

It seemed a long time before Anita answered. Gradually small sounds from outside percolated into the silence—the chirping of sparrows, distant traffic and the eerie shriek of a diesel train. As the others waited patiently, Anita got up and went over to the window. It was with her back turned that she answered Jenny. 'I always thought I had strong views too—against it, I mean. But it's different when you're actually faced with the decision.'

'It stops being theoretical and becomes horribly real,' Laura said sympathetically. 'Does that mean you've decided to apply for a termination? You

haven't got very far and I should think this would
be the ideal time to have it done.'

Again Anita was silent. Then she swung round
and faced them defiantly. 'Yes, I have. Taking it
by and large I feel it's the best thing. After all, it
doesn't really seem like a baby yet and it will all be
so easy I shall hardly feel I've had anything done
at all.'

'I think you've made the right decision,' Jenny
said gently. 'Don't you, Laura?'

'Whatever Anita decided would be right for her.'
She forced a note of cheerfulness into her voice.
'Didn't you invite us here for coffee, Jenny?'

When Jenny had left the room to make it, the
other two sat in silence, each busy with her own
thoughts. Laura's mind had flown back to her spell
of duty in the obstetrics ward not very long ago.
Mr O'Neill, the consultant in charge, was a fiery
little man, apt to express himself with great force,
though kindness itself when the circumstances
justified it. His views on the termination of a
pregnancy were well known to his nurses. He did
not utterly condemn it but would not grant permission easily. There had to be some very good
reason, preferably a medical one rather than
psychological.

How would Anita fare when she made her
request?

The girls did not discuss the matter again that
evening and separated as soon as they had drunk
their coffee. Laura did not sleep for some time, in

spite of her tiredness. At first she thought about
Anita's news and then about Sister Leggett who,
though she had stood up well to the operation,
had been seriously ill all day.

After that she allowed the thoughts which she
had been holding at bay to enter her mind and
take possession. Over and over again she relived
those moments with Martin before the telephone
summoned him to the hospital.

He had kissed her before and the effect on her
emotions had been devastating, but somehow last
night had been different. Last night, in spite of her
frantic attempts to evade the truth, she had been
obliged to face up for the first time to the fact that
she loved him.

There could be no future in that at all. Absolutely none.

Her pillow was still wet with tears in the morning but an iron resolution seemed to have taken
possession of her soul. There must be no more of
what Martin obviously looked on as light-hearted
dalliance; in future, she would at all costs avoid
being alone with him. That way she would surely
eventually manage to uproot from her heart the
man who thought nothing of amusing himself
with another girl while—probably—engaged to
someone else.

She was glad to be on early duty and plunged
whole-heartedly into work.

'The news about Sister is better this morning,'
Acting Sister Mildmay told her, 'and I think the

prognosis is reasonably good. She's pretty tough, you know. I wouldn't be surprised if she comes back to work and carries on until she's sixty.'

'I rather hope she does. She'll probably be a lot easier to work with now she's got rid of her ulcer.'

'I'm afraid we're going to be short-staffed.' The midwife grimaced at the pile of paperwork on her desk. 'They're going to try and get another midwife to help out, but with the holiday season beginning it won't be easy.'

The morning passed like a flash but with everything under control. When Laura went to lunch she found Anita in the canteen, sitting alone and staring into space, and had no hesitation in joining her.

'I've fixed up to see Mr O'Neill,' the girl told her. 'In two days' time.'

'At the clinic?'

Anita nodded. 'He's going to let me in before he deals with his patients. I don't suppose it'll take long.'

'You'll be glad when it's over,' Laura sympathised.

'You can say that again!' She pushed the salad on her plate about with her fork but made no attempt to eat it. 'I've got a free afternoon today and so has Jenny. She's persuaded me to go round the shops with her but I don't want to a bit. How can I look at summer dresses when I don't know if I shall be needing to buy maternity gear before long?'

There was no answer to that and Laura attempted none. After a moment Anita continued speaking. 'She wants us to have tea at the Granville, meaning it to be a—a treat. It's so kind of
her and I just couldn't say I can't face food just now.'

Ever since her birthday lunch, Laura had mentally connected the Granville with Lucy's pregnancy and she didn't want to be reminded of it. Neither did she envy her two friends their tour of the shops. In her present mood it was work she wanted and plenty of it.

She spent most of her own afternoon in the delivery-room where a young mother was giving birth to twins. The babies, both girls, were born ten minutes apart and Mrs Redfern's first thought was to enquire whether they were identical.

The midwife looked down at the yelling infant she had just delivered and compared her with the one Laura was holding. 'It's hard to tell at this stage but I'd say it's very probable. Did you want them to be identical?'

'Oh, yes. I was an identical twin myself and it's marvellous to have such a special relationship with someone exactly one's own age.'

'It can lead to complications,' the father said cautiously.

Laura left them discussing it and took the babies out to make them look presentable. She had just finished and was tucking the infants, warmly wrapped in shawls, into the curve of her arms when the door opened and Martin came in. It was hardly possible to bolt back to the delivery-room, specially as it turned out he had come for the express purpose of seeing the twins.

'I've just finished my clinic and Jonathan mentioned you'd got twins in the ward.' He came closer and touched a little dark head with his finger. 'Nice babies. I gather they're OK?'

'Very much so.' Her pulses racing, she looked down at her burden, and the wide blue eyes apparently stared up into her face.

'I would think they're identical, wouldn't you?' Martin went on conversationally.

'Yes.' She ventured a glance at his face and lowered her eyes again quickly. 'I—I must hurry back with them. The parents are waiting.'

Seeing him so unexpectedly like that had done something disastrous to her poise. Closing the door behind her, she took a deep breath, fastened a smile to her face, and approached the bed. As she had expected, the next few minutes were happy ones.

She was off duty early that day, having worked through from early morning. Glad to be alone, she drove home slowly, unaccountably tired.

It would be summer next month and her mother and father would be expecting her for a visit. With a sudden passionate intensity she wished it could be sooner—next week perhaps—so that she could escape from the exquisite pain of seeing Martin almost daily. Perhaps in the quietness of her home village she could come to terms with an utterly hopeless love and learn to live with it until it died a natural death.

If it ever did.

CHAPTER TEN

MR O'NEILL's clinic was on a Thursday. That morning Laura woke up with her mind full of Anita's ordeal and she reflected, with a wry inward smile, that it made a change from her own troubles. She just wished it didn't have to be one of her friends who had provided her with something else to think about.

They met by chance as they approached the hospital to report for early duty. Anita's skin was pale and her large dark eyes full of melancholy. 'I don't know how I'm going to get through the morning,' she said. 'I'm so afraid I shall make some awful mistake in the ward.'

'Of course you won't.' Laura did her best to sound encouraging. 'You're far too experienced a nurse to do that.'

'I hope you're right.' Anita sighed. 'If Mr O'Neill does agree to the termination, do you think he'll do it at once—like tomorrow?' Laura had no idea. As she hesitated, Anita went on speaking without waiting for a reply. 'It would be marvellously convenient if he did do it tomorrow because I've got a free weekend and——'

'So have I. Are you intending to go home to your parents?'

'No. I don't feel a bit like facing the family just now, whatever the verdict this afternoon.'

They had reached the side-door into the hospital which they normally used. In a moment they would separate and go to their wards.

'Just a minute.' Laura put her hand on her friend's arm. 'I've had an idea. If you're at a loose end this weekend, why don't you come and stay at my cottage? I'm not doing anything special and I'd love to have you. We could go out in the car— take a picnic and——'

'Oh, Laura—I'd love that!' Anita's eyes brightened. 'I was dreading having to stay at the hospital if Mr O'Neill refuses, and even if he doesn't he may not operate immediately. Are you sure you want me to come?'

'Of course I'm sure, you twit! Let me know how things go this afternoon and then we'll make arrangements.'

Walking down the covered way which led to the maternity block, she suddenly remembered that her spare-room wasn't properly furnished. But at least there was a bed and she had a spare duvet, so maybe Anita wouldn't mind about there being very little else. In her present tensed-up state she might not even notice the bareness.

Laura snatched a moment during the morning to tell Jenny about the invitation.

'That's a good idea. She'll be your first visitor, won't she?' Jenny commented.

'Yes, but I'm not really ready for visitors yet. It

was a sudden impulse.' She picked up a yelling baby, expertly wrapped it in a shawl and set off in the direction of the waiting mother.

They had no further opportunity for private conversation until after lunch, when the ward was quiet and most of the mothers taking a nap before their visitors arrived.

'I wonder when we'll know what Mr O'Neill said to Anita?' Laura's voice sounded as anxious as she felt.

'I told her to come along to my room as soon as she was off duty this evening,' Jenny said. 'She's in such a terrible state, poor thing. She's been sleep-walking—did you know she was subject to that when things are getting her down?'

Laura shook her head. 'How did you find out?'

'I woke up in the middle of the night feeling hungry, and I remembered I'd got a slice of cheesecake in the fridge, so I went along to get it and on the way I met Anita in her nightie. I said something to her and she didn't take the slightest notice. It scared me a bit until I realised she was *asleep*.'

'So what did you do?'

'Led her back to bed, of course. She didn't offer any resistance. In the morning I thought I'd better mention it and she told me about doing it occasionally.'

'She's certainly got enough to worry about at the moment!'

Jenny grimaced in agreement. 'You'll come along too this evening, won't you?'

'Just try and stop me!' Laura dredged up a laugh. 'But I don't know what we're going to say to her if she hasn't succeeded in getting a termination.'

They were both in a state of nervous tension when they went off duty together at eight o'clock and walked over to the nurses' home. There was no sign of Anita and they had had plenty of time for fruitless discussion before she appeared, more than half an hour late.

'Been working overtime?' Jenny asked. 'I expect you could do with some coffee.'

'No, thanks. I've just had some with Gavin.' Looking utterly exhausted, Anita collapsed into a chair.

Studying her anxiously, Laura tried to guess what her news would be. She wasn't looking cheerful, but the situation—whichever way you viewed it—wasn't a very happy one in any case.

'We wondered what had happened to you,' she ventured. 'I suppose we might have guessed you were with Gavin.'

Anita raised her head and glanced from one to the other. 'I've been arguing with him ever since I came off duty and it's just about torn me apart.' She paused and then added bleakly, 'Coming on top of what happened this afternoon.'

There was a brief pause and then Jenny said

cautiously, 'Do you mean when you saw Mr
O'Neill?'

'Yes.' Anita drew a long quivering breath. 'He
won't do it. He was so horrible to me that I cried.'

Laura got up impulsively and went to kneel on
the floor close to her. 'How absolutely awful for
you! I *am* sorry.'

'I do think it was mean of him to treat you like
that,' Jenny said indignantly. 'I'd like to tell him
just what I think of him.'

'It wouldn't do any good.' Anita smiled wanly.
'He certainly wouldn't change his mind. And you
shouldn't be too hard on him anyway, Jenny,
because he suddenly altered when I burst into
tears and was quite nice and kind. He advised me
to have the baby and told me I was lucky my
boyfriend wanted to marry me.'

'So what are you going to do?'

'I don't know. Gavin still thinks we should get
married but I haven't really changed my mind
about it not being right for us. I thought it was all
settled when I decided to ask for a termination and
now it isn't settled at all.'

They talked for some time, getting nowhere at
all, and then Anita went off to bed.

'I feel terribly sorry for her,' Jenny sighed.

'So do I.' Laura got up from her uncomfortable
position on the floor. 'But there's nothing you or I
can do to help.'

'You're doing something by offering her a peaceful weekend away from the hospital. It's what she

needs. Maybe by Monday she'll have got it clear in her mind.'

Nothing warned them—not even the smallest premonition—that by Monday Anita would have had her problem solved for her.

The two girls drove out to Mayes together on Friday evening. It was warm and still sunny, and the chestnut trees along one side of the green were bedecked in their early summer finery. In the cottage gardens lilac sweetened the air and a few rambler roses were in bloom.

As Laura inserted her key into the lock, she could hear the telephone ringing.

'I hope that's not Gavin,' Anita said nervously. 'He said he might ring up and I told him not to. I'm trying to keep a clear head this weekend and he muddles me.'

'You go and sit down while I answer it. It's probably not him at all.'

But it was Gavin. He said urgently, 'There's something wrong with your phone, Laura. This is the third time I've tried to get through——'

'We've only just come in.'

'Both the other times the phone suddenly stopped ringing without anybody answering it. You ought to report it.'

'I will in the morning if it's still misbehaving. There's a public phone-box outside the shop. Er—did you want to talk to Anita?'

'Well, of course I do.' He sounded aggrieved. 'Will you tell her, please?'

Laura hesitated, anxious not to interfere and yet impatient with him because he didn't seem to have the sense to leave his girlfriend alone to do her thinking in peace. She said diffidently, 'Couldn't it wait until Monday? She really does want to be left to work things out for herself——' There was a click and the line went dead. It was as though the telephone had taken matters into its own hands and decided to put an end to the conversation. Half hoping that it would remain out of order for a while, Laura went to report to Anita and was not surprised when she seemed relieved that they were cut off from the hospital world.

'He can't come over here to talk to me,' she said, 'because he's on call.'

They spent a lazy evening, eating a leisurely meal, watching television, not talking very much. The quietness of the village wrapped round them and Laura thought she could actually see her guest unwinding. It was only ten-thirty when they went to bed and Anita announced that she believed she would sleep for the first time for several nights.

Laura lay awake for a short time and then slipped into deep, restful slumber. For two hours she remained totally unaware, and then—quite suddenly—she was wide awake.

At first she didn't know what had roused her. Some sound perhaps? Rubbing her eyes, she yawned and turned over with the intention of drifting off again. But then she heard it once more and this time she was sufficiently conscious to recognise the sound. Footsteps on the landing.

Probably it was Anita going down to the bathroom, she reasoned. At Lavender Cottage the bathroom was downstairs, built out at the back, as in so many other modernised country cottages. Satisfied that she had solved the problem, Laura again composed herself for sleep.

The next moment she was sitting up in bed, her heart pounding as her hand stretched out for the bedside light. That terrible dull thud could have only one meaning even though there had been no human sound to accompany it, no cry of terror— nothing but an eerie silence.

Out on the landing, Laura switched on the light and gazed fearfully down the short flight of steep stairs. Anita lay in a heap at the bottom, her head against the door leading into the kitchen, and it must have been the noise made when she crashed into it which Laura had heard.

She went down the stairs so fast that she was in danger of falling herself, and yet there was still time to wonder why Anita hadn't put on a light. She hadn't needed to grope her way down in the dark.

Suddenly something Jenny had told her flashed into her mind. Anita had a history of sleep-walking. Was that what she had been doing tonight?

Down on her knees by the prone body, Laura touched the limbs cautiously but could not decide whether arms or legs were likely to be broken. What was quite certain was the fact that Anita was unconscious and might easily have fractured her skull. Scrambling to her feet, she went straight to the phone, and as she did so she remembered it had been out of order that afternoon. But perhaps only incoming calls had been affected. That sort of thing had been known to happen. Sending up a small silent prayer, she dialled the hospital number.

There was no sound at the other end, no small clickings—nothing at all in her ears except the beating of her own heart.

Shivering with cold and shock, Laura stood there in her thin nightdress and debated what to do. First she must go back to Anita and find out if there were any signs of returning consciousness.

She lay in the same cramped position, still totally unaware of what had happened, and with any luck she would remain unconscious until help could be summoned. Stepping over her carefully, Laura raced upstairs and began to dress frantically, pulling on jeans and a sweater and thrusting her bare feet into trainers. Her mind worked furiously, making plans and then rejecting them.

Both her neighbours had telephones but they were elderly people and would take a lot of time to rouse. The call-box by the shop was the obvious place but she couldn't possibly go all that way unless she took the car.

Much nearer—and therefore quicker—was the telephone at Hill House.

Lucy's? Laura hesitated and then decided against ringing the front doorbell. It might take ages to wake her and get her to the door, in addition to alarming her considerably. Much better to go to Martin's door. Doctors were used to being disturbed in the night and always responded much more rapidly than other people.

And so Laura did what she had wanted to do all along, though she hadn't admitted it to herself. She ran all the way to Hill House and rang the bell of the granny flat.

'What the devil's the matter?' Martin, his dark hair on end and his arms thrust into a crimson towelling robe, stood in the doorway and stared at her.

She was panting so much she couldn't speak, and he put out a hand and drew her into the tiny hall. 'Take it easy,' he advised. 'Nothing's so urgent—except cardiac arrest—that it can't wait a few seconds.' His voice sharpened. 'It's not that, I hope?'

'No.' Laura drew a deep breath and willed her thudding heart to slow down. 'It's Anita—she's fallen downstairs and my phone's out of order.'

'Anita?'

'She's a staff nurse—a friend of mine—and she's staying with me for the weekend. I think she was sleep-walking.'

Martin was already on his way to the telephone. 'Is she conscious?' he asked over his shoulder.

'Not when I left. I don't think she'll come round very quickly. She gave her head a very severe bash.'

She heard him at the phone, asking for an ambulance, and then he reappeared briefly. 'I'll fling some clothes on and then come back with you. Sit down, Laura, and try to relax. Everything's under control now.'

It was wonderful to hand over responsibility to him and know that she need make no more decisions. Wonderful, too, to have him with her when she returned to her house. She tried to persuade herself it was because of having moral support but all the time she knew it was much, much more than that.

Anita lay as she had left her and Martin made a careful but necessarily cursory examination. 'Fractures of the tib and fib on the right leg,' he reported, 'and I'm pretty sure she'll have broken some ribs. It's her head I'm most concerned about, but only an X-ray will show whether she's fractured her skull.'

'She might have broken her neck,' Laura said soberly.

'Yes, but I don't think she has.' Martin touched her arm. 'Come into the sitting-room to wait for the ambulance. There's nothing you can do here.'

He was standing very close and, even in the midst of her desperate anxiety, Laura felt her senses responding to his maleness. Like her he was wearing jeans and a shapeless sweater coming well below the hips and making his body anonymous, yet with every fibre of her being she was aware of him.

'There *is* something I've got to do,' she said tautly. 'I must pack Anita's case with her toilet things and—and anything else she's likely to need in hospital.'

'Better be quick, then.' He thrust his hands into his pockets and went to stare out of the window.

Laura had everything ready just in time. She watched while the ambulancemen gently, and with infinite care, straightened the crumpled figure sufficiently to lift it on to the stretcher. They were loading Anita into the ambulance when Martin approached and spoke quietly in Laura's ear. 'Aren't you going with her?'

'I'm going to follow in my car. I shall need it for getting back.'

'I'm sure you'd much rather go in the ambulance. I'll bring you home.'

She stared at him, her eyes dilating slightly in the lights. '*You*? But there's no need for you to come.'

'Perhaps not, but I'm certainly not letting you drive after the shock you've just had. And for God's sake don't start arguing!' he added explosively. 'Hop in quickly and I'll go and get my car.'

Meekly, Laura obeyed. He'd be used to ordering Lucy about, she reasoned, and probably thought all women appreciated being taken charge of, though she had made it plain more than once that she personally detested it.

Sitting beside Anita and keeping an anxious eye on her condition, she found her mind going off on a different track. Supposing that Martin's tendency to take charge was based on something which had no connection with mere bossiness, wouldn't she view it in quite a different light?

If it was based on love, for instance. . .

Laura sighed and thrust the thought away. She must be crazy to let herself imagine even for one moment that there could ever be love between herself and Martin.

They were approaching the hospital and the A & E Department, alerted by him that a nurse was in trouble, were ready for them. Anita was whisked off to a cubicle and Laura turned forlornly away and went to find Martin sitting in his car outside.

They did not speak on the short drive back to Mayes. When they reached Lavender Cottage, he took her key from her and unlocked the door. Pale under the outside light, her eyes lost in deep pits of shadow, she gazed up at him wordlessly.

Martin put his hands on her shoulders. 'Try not to worry too much,' he said gently. 'I think I can promise you that Anita's going to be all right. The best thing you can do is make yourself a hot drink and then go back to bed and get some sleep.'

He was doing it again—telling her what to do.

But this time Laura didn't mind. She was too tired for argument, too tired for anything except being taken care of. 'I'll do that,' she agreed, 'and thank you for all you've done. I'm very grateful.'

He muttered something which sounded like, 'I don't want your gratitude,' pulled her closer with unnecessary violence and dropped a kiss on the top of her head. A moment later she was inside the house, without knowing quite how she had got there, and the door had been closed firmly behind her.

Although she obediently made herself a drink, getting to sleep again was every bit as difficult as she had anticipated. Her mind seemed to have become a roundabout of unrelated thoughts— Anita's accident, her own love for Martin, and a multitude of trivial worries, which in daylight would seem unimportant, jostled for attention until every nerve in her body was quivering. She fell asleep at last and slept late in the morning.

Her first thought was for Anita and, without waiting for breakfast, Laura started up her car and drove to the public phone-box. Having reported that her own phone was out of order, she rang up the hospital and asked for the Sick Bay.

By a lucky chance, the nurse who answered was someone she knew fairly well and she was able to ask for details as freely as though she were a relative. These turned out to be much the same as Martin had predicted.

'Four broken ribs, fractured tib and fib and

concussion,' the nurse said crisply. 'Also numerous bruises, of course.'

'No fractured skull?'

'Her head took a terrific knock but she's OK.' She hesitated and then added, 'She's been haemorrhaging——'

'I wondered if that would happen.'

'Did you? Well, it's over and done with now, but Anita doesn't know yet. We shan't say anything about it unless she asks, but perhaps you can give me a hint as to what her reaction is likely to be? I know you're a great friend of hers.'

There was no hesitation in Laura's reply. 'I think you'll find she's greatly relieved.'

She replaced the receiver slowly, her mind still on the conversation. So Anita had lost her baby. By her fall down the stairs she had achieved what Mr O'Neill had denied her, though what the outcome would be was anybody's guess. Anita and Gavin would have to work that out for themselves.

CHAPTER ELEVEN

NEVER had a precious free weekend seemed so long. Laura did some gardening, made a cake, and rearranged the furniture in her sitting-room. By lunchtime on Sunday she was wishing she could go back on duty and deliver a few babies. That way she could keep her wayward thoughts in order.

The morning had been cloudy with a hint of rain, but at noon the sky lightened and the sun burst forth, making the countryside look so beautiful that it seemed criminal not to be enjoying it.

She was just finishing a sketchy lunch and wondering whether she could summon up the energy to cut the grass, when the phone rang. Apparently Telecom had repaired it without needing to visit.

To her surprise it was Lucy.

'I'm ringing to ask when you and your friends are going to start using my swimming-pool,' she said after they had exchanged greetings. 'The weather is quite warm now and, in any case, it's heated. If you're not doing anything special this afternoon, why don't you come over? I'm sure you could rustle up somebody to come with you.'

Laura instantly panicked. Martin would probably be there on a Sunday. Much as the prospect of a swim appealed to her, she simply dared not risk it. 'Jenny's on duty all day,' she said quickly, 'and Anita fell downstairs so she's hospitalised——'

'I heard about that. How is she?'

'As well as can be expected.' Laura smiled as she used the well-worn expression. 'I think she's going to be all right.'

'I'm so glad.' Lucy sounded genuinely pleased. 'Well, if you can't think of anybody else to invite, why don't you come over by yourself? I'm afraid I shan't be here, though. I've promised to take the boys to the sea—Lorraine too, of course, but she's hardly up to making sandcastles yet!' There was a pause and then she added casually, 'Martin isn't here either so you'd be all on your own. Can you swim?'

'Oh, yes—I'm quite a strong swimmer.'

'That's OK, then. You'd be quite safe.' Again she paused. 'How about it?'

Laura hesitated, still reluctant to accept the invitation, but the early summer afternoon stretched emptily before her and she knew it would move even more slowly than the morning had done. 'I really intended to do some more gardening,' she explained, 'but if I can clear it with my conscience, perhaps I will come over.'

'Don't be too hard on yourself!' Lucy laughed. 'You're supposed to have fun on your free weekend, aren't you? Just because your friend fell downstairs, you don't have to slave all the time.'

Laura made polite noises and the conversation ended. She still hadn't committed herself, but the prospect of doing something different began to seem more and more attractive. Suddenly her mind was made up. She would go over to Hill House and do her utmost to enjoy her solitary swim.

It wasn't until she was getting ready that it occurred to her to wonder how Lucy knew she had a free weekend. She must have mentioned it to Martin when he drove her back from the hospital after Anita had been admitted, though she had no recollection of it.

There seemed to be no reason why he should have told Lucy. Laura puzzled over it for a moment and dismissed it with a shrug since it was obviously of no importance.

Ten minutes later she was walking up the drive of Hill House. It was very quiet and even the birds seemed to be taking a Sunday afternoon nap. For some reason she felt uneasy, as though the rows of tall windows were staring at her in disapproval. What was she doing here? they seemed to be asking. Didn't she know she was trespassing?

It was so absurd that Laura felt quite annoyed with herself and marched resolutely round the side of the house, past Martin's front door and into the large back garden. The pool lay before her, blue and shining in the sunlight, beautiful and tempting. There was a paved area all round it, with plants in tubs and white-painted chairs and tables, and, on the far side, a small building evidently intended for undressing.

Laura didn't need it. She was wearing her new one-piece jade green swimming-costume under her jeans and T-shirt. Slipping off her outer clothing, she stepped to the edge and stood poised— a slender figure with her gold cap of hair shining and her long legs, lightly tanned, bare to the hips. Taking a deep breath, she dived in and began to swim strongly up and down.

It was gloriously refreshing at first, but after a while she began to feel a little bored without someone to race against, or splash, or practise diving with, so she climbed out, spread out her towel and lay stretched out in the sun. Deliciously relaxed, she half closed her eyes.

Perhaps she dozed a little. Certainly she didn't hear the sound of a car engine, but something made her open her eyes wide and sit upright, every inch of her taut with nervous tension.

The tall lean figure of a man was coming towards the pool, sauntering casually in the sunlight, his muscular body clad in the briefest of swimming-trunks.

Laura gave one horrified look and, acting entirely by instinct, rolled over and into the pool, disappearing beneath the water with scarcely a splash. She swam a few strokes submerged and then surfaced, already regretting her ridiculous behaviour. Continuing towards the far end of the pool, she debated what to do. There didn't seem to be many options and she ended by lingering at the deep end, holding the rail with one hand and letting her limbs float lazily.

Martin had wasted no time and was already swimming towards her, his windmill arms giving only occasional glimpses of his dark head. He was certainly a magnificent swimmer and it was impossible not to admire his style and speed.

He stopped a few yards away and, treading water, gave her a casual glance. 'Want to have a race?' he asked.

'No, thanks! I wouldn't stand a chance. As a matter of fact——' she swallowed nervously '—I've done quite a lot of swimming this afternoon and I'm very out of practice, so I think I'd better get dressed now. . .' Her voice died away as she remembered that she had omitted to bring any underclothes. The pants didn't matter so much since she had jeans, but her T-shirt was very thin and would show every detail of her breasts without a bra. The alternative was to pull on her clothes over the wet bathing-suit. She had just made up her mind to bear the discomfort when Martin spoke again.

'You were sunbathing when I arrived so why don't you dry off again before dressing? It saves so much trouble.'

'Oh—er—yes, perhaps I will,' Laura said feebly. Swimming back to the shallow end, she scolded herself for not sticking to her intention. The trouble was that part of her—the crazy, treacherous part which didn't know how to be sensible—wanted so desperately to stay longer that it would not be denied.

She reached the steps and hauled herself up them, a brilliant figure in the tight-fitting, bright green suit slashed to the waist at the back and with only a narrow strip between armpits and hips. Scattering drops of water, she sat down on the towel and, quite unable to relax, remained rigidly upright, watching Martin swimming up and down as though he were aiming at the Olympics.

Perhaps it was the warmth of the sun, but gradually Laura's tenseness left her. She even dared to lie down and close her eyes.

When she opened them again, Martin was standing before her, water streaming from him and his hair on end. He said tersely, 'Is there room for me on that towel? I forgot to bring one and I can't go in dripping like this.'

'It's quite a big towel.' Laura moved to the extreme edge and went on nervously, 'The sun's lovely and warm. We shall soon be dry.'

Martin ignored the conversational opening. Stretched out beside her, so close that every nerve in her body was aware of him, he turned his head towards her. She could feel his eyes on her face but she refused to meet them.

To break the silence which had suddenly become charged with something she couldn't give a name to, Laura said the first thing which came into her head. 'Lucy said you weren't here today.'

'I wasn't this morning. I was playing squash with my registrar and we had a pub lunch together.' He paused and then added bitterly, 'No doubt if you'd known I might be here you wouldn't have come.'

It was so manifestly true that Laura floundered. Trying to find some way of softening her agreement, she ended up with a vague murmur which Martin ignored. 'It was a real lucky break finding you sunbathing beside the pool,' he continued. 'You couldn't run away, as you so often do, wearing nothing but that extremely provocative swim-suit. I can't help wondering whether Lucy hoped I might turn up this afternoon.'

'Lucy! But—but why should she?' Laura's head was spinning.

'She knew I wanted to talk to you.'

'I don't understand.' In her agitation, she sat up and stared down at him. 'Why should Lucy want to give you a chance to talk to me?' She waved her hands wildly. 'None of it makes any sense. I thought you and she were—well, sort of engaged.'

'You what? Where on earth did you get that idea?'

'We all thought it——'

His brows drew together angrily. 'My private affairs have been discussed by all and sundry?'

'No, no, of course not. It was only Jenny and

me.' Laura's heart had begun to thump so power-fully that she had difficulty in continuing, but she managed to gasp out, 'Isn't it true, then? You aren't going to marry Lucy?'

'No, I'm not. I'm very fond of her—in fact, she was my first girlfriend, if you really want to know—but she's in love with someone else, a bloke who's working abroad just now but he'll be home in a couple of months.' And he added, apparently as an afterthought, 'He's Lorraine's father.'

'Oh!' Her mind in a turmoil, she could think of nothing to add.

'I can't think why you imagined such a load of rubbish. I should have thought I'd made the way I feel about you pretty obvious on more than one occasion——'

'You made it pretty plain you thought I was a fool—someone who needed constant bossing before she could be trusted to do anything properly——'

Martin jerked into a sitting position, his bare shoulder touching Laura's. 'You really believed that?' he demanded incredulously.

'Yes, I did—and still do!' Laura faced him boldly, her eyes blazing because, if she didn't whip up her anger, she wasn't sure what might happen.

But when she saw the hurt in his, her gaze dropped and instead of being furious she wanted to cry.

'No wonder you were always running away

from me.' There was pain and bitterness in his voice. 'You surely do cut a man down to size, Laura.'

'I didn't mean——'

'Yes, you did, and it's better to be honest.' Martin paused and then continued slowly. 'Maybe there's not much point in it, but I want to be honest too, and that means I'm going to tell you how much I love you, whether you're interested or not.' He took her hands and held them tightly. 'I learnt to love you while working with you—I used to watch your tenderness with the babies and the understanding way you treated the mums. And I want more than anything else in the world to marry you and take care of you for always.'

She tried to speak but emotion choked her and, before she could think what to say, Martin went on urgently. 'I've *got* to know how you feel about me—whether there's any hope.' His hands on her shoulders, he turned her to face him, his eyes raking her face. 'I shan't let you go until you tell me.'

'I—I'm still in a state of shock. I think perhaps I'm afraid to believe what you've been saying——'

'Afraid?' The dark brows rose incredulously. 'Would you find it easier to believe if I told you again? I love you, my dear, darling, exasperating girl, and it's real love I'm talking about—the sort that wants to get married and set up a home. *Now* will you tell me if I can dare to hope?'

'Oh, Martin!' Laura flung away all her doubts
and fears. Now she could admit, not only in the
secrecy of her own heart but in words too, how
much she had longed for his love. 'I can offer you
something much, much better than hope, My love
is all yours, Martin, and I give it freely, here and
now.'

He started to speak but she laid a finger on his
lips. 'I struggled not to let myself love you because
of Lucy, but it wasn't much good. And when I
said I was afraid to believe you, it was because I
wanted to so desperately.'

For a long moment Martin held her gaze and
she saw incredulity turn to joy. 'Oh, my
darling——' his voice was hoarse with feeling
'—for a moment I was afraid too, but I'm not
now—not the least little bit.'

Laura lay down again and held out her arms. As
she felt the hard pressure of his mouth and the
strength of his near-naked body, she understood
that the time for words was past. Her own body
was speaking for her and she knew with a glorious
certainty that what was going to happen was
utterly right for them both.

And so, in the privacy of Lucy's garden,
shielded by trees and bushes from the curious
stares of neighbours, they put the seal on their
love and taught each other the true meaning of
happiness.

Life and death drama in this gripping new novel of passion and suspense

Following a vicious attack on a tough property developer and his beautiful wife, eminent surgeon David Compton fought fiercely to save both lives, little knowing just how deeply he would become involved in a complex web of deadly revenge. Ginette Irving, the cool and practical theatre sister, was an enigma to David, but could he risk an affair with the worrying threat to his career and now the sinister attempts on his life?

W●RLDWIDE

Price: £3.99   Published: May 1991

Available from Boots, Martins, John Menzies, W.H. Smith, Woolworths and other paperback stockists.

Also available from Mills and Boon Reader Service, P.O. Box 236, Thornton Road, Croydon, Surrey CR9 3RU

Three women, three loves . . . Haunted by one dark, forbidden secret.

ALIX ATKINSON

Boundaries

Margaret – a corner of her heart would always remain Karl's, but now she had to reveal the secrets of their passion which still had the power to haunt and disturb.

Miriam – the child of that forbidden love, hurt by her mother's little love for her, had been seduced by Israel's magic and the love of a special man.

Hannah – blonde and delicate, was the child of that love and in her blue eyes, Margaret could again see Karl.

It was for the girl's sake that the truth had to be told, for only by confessing the secrets of the past could Margaret give Hannah hope for the future.

— MEDICAL ROMANCE —

The books for your enjoyment this month are:

HEART SEARCHING Sara Burton
DOCTOR TRANSFORMED Marion Lennox
LOVING CARE Margaret Barker
LOVE YOUR NEIGHBOUR Clare Lavenham

Treats in store!

Watch next month for the following absorbing stories:

GIVE ME TOMORROW Sarah Franklin
SPECIALIST IN LOVE Sharon Wirdnam
LOVE AND DR ADAMS Judith Hunte
THE CHALLENGE OF DR BLAKE Lilian Darcy

Available from Boots, Martins, John Menzies, W.H. Smith, Woolworths and other paperback stockists.

Also available from Mills and Boon Reader Service, P.O. Box 236, Thornton Road, Croydon, Surrey CR9 3RU.

Readers in South Africa — write to:
Independent Book Services Pty, Postbag X3010, Randburg, 2125, S. Africa.